CREEL 5

MUSCALIET

PUBLISHED BY MUSCALIET ON BEHALF OF THE UNIVERSITY OF ESSEX

Department of Literature, Film and Theatre Studies, 5NW.6.16, University of Essex, Wivenhoe Park, Colchester, Essex, CO4 3SQ, United Kingdom
www.muscaliet.co.uk

First published 2020 in paperback

Editor-in-Chief: Ezgi Gürhan

Associate Editors: Hannah Bransom, Loren Ennis, Simon Everett, Saffron Forde, Sam 'Jesta' Geden, Fanny Haushalter, Sophie Jeans, Jennifer Li, Cristina del Pozo Huertas, Tal Rejwan, Melissa Shales, Minn Yap

Cover image by Tal Rejwan

Typeset in Adobe Garamond Pro

ISBN 978-1-912616-08-4

Creel 5

An anthology of creative writing

Contents

Elizabeth Kuti

Foreword

It's spring 2020, in the midst of the coronavirus lockdown — and we have never needed creative writing so badly. *Creel 5*, the annual anthology created by students at the University of Essex, enters the world in an April that, despite its blues skies and blossom, has never felt this cruel before. Banished to our houses, instructed not to go out unless we must, and if we must, to keep two meters away from anyone else, this is not so much the 'showres soote' of Chaucer's April pilgrims, but Winston Smith's bright, cold dystopia where the clocks are striking thirteen.

Bounded in our nutshells, it is some comfort at least, that of all the pleasures denied to us right now – company, touch, holidays, laughter, shared food and drink, games, theatre, cinema — at least the pleasures of the imagination remain. If art is cheap travel, then a facility for writing is a ticket around the world, and into space and time, with an open return date. The writers in this anthology — all at different stages of their writing lives — have exploited this mental and artistic freedom to the hilt. On the theme of collisions, the encounters here range from epic clashes in the struggle for Troy, or on the battlefields of the First World War; to internal psychological collisions with loss, or despair, with love, with identity crisis — even with autism. Perhaps 'collision' of one kind of another, is at the heart of all impulses to write, as the mind tests out its boundaries, hammers at the walls that hem us in, and takes a running jump at all the forces that fan our desire by containing us and putting obstacles in the way of our needs and wishes. Language is the tool we use to chip at the walls of the prison. Sometimes the simplest of phrases resonates the most; Karenza Bolton's,

> Somewhere between
> Okay and crying
> Dying, dying

Or Ezgi Gürhan's penetrating thoughts on classical mythic figures:

> Oh, Medusa
> Did they fear you
> Because your hair
> Is no longer tame?

The collisions crafted into language in this collection are erotic, artistic, or even as in Petra McQueen's haunting prose piece, a psychic smashing-together of time and space in the midst of that most literal of collisions, war.

To browse this collection is to be offered a warm slice of intense life — shared intimacies of thought and feeling — all the more precious for the fractured separation we are all enduring right now. To write a poem about isolation is to relieve a little bit of my loneliness, through the words you have found to express it. Writing is always a reaching out. The students of the Department of Literature, Film and Theatre studies at Essex who created this volume, as writers, editors, and makers, came together in a shared endeavour to capture what we are feeling now, and to make a book that holds these complexities with beauty and craftsmanship. They have accomplished this with care, precision, teamwork, and attention to detail. I am profoundly grateful to all of them, and to Simon Everett, poet, author, and editor of Muscaliet Press, for his leadership of this inaugural publishing project, along with the indefatigable Melissa Shales — both, I am proud to say, alumni of the department — both sharing their gifts and hard-won expertise with generosity, amongst a new generation of Essex writers.

April is the month of green shoots, of unfurling, and the promise of sunnier days ahead — and so it is an appropriate moment to welcome *Creel 5* into our current world of uncertain hibernation, and to send this anthology out into the world, its words unfurling like opening buds: a lovingly-crafted testament to the human spirit that mourns the fractures with words and stories, and out of brokenness, makes a mosaic.

Professor Elizabeth Kuti
Head of Department
Literature, Film and Theatre Studies, University of Essex
Wivenhoe; April 2020

Tom Allpress

Untitled

I
Am
Now
Ever
Bound
Toward
Another
Meteoric
Collision.
Shattering,
Melodramatic,
Astronomical
Schizophrenia,
Emphatically
Overwrought.
Shimmering
Celestial
Confetti,
Falling
Silent.
Smoke.
Fade
Out
On
I.

Tom Allpress

Turn the Wheel

I'm just sitting here, safe,
Eyes facing forward.
My face a picture of calm.
Nothing to see here.

I grip the wheel
and think what if I…
turned it suddenly,
Or put my foot down hard?

There'd be no-one to shout at me,
No-one to tell me I'm wrong.
There would be
no-one.

I think of blood;
The smell of it,
Mixed with metal and petrol;
What it would taste like.

I could turn the wheel,
Or put my foot down hard;
Really give them a show.
Then they'll see.

Tom Allpress

Millions

The millions gather,
In a vast, dark tunnel,
Like cattle,
Mute and unsuspecting.

The great machine fires up,
(...)
The dark rumbles,
(....)
The millions grow agitated,
(.....)
Heat fills the tunnel
and

The dark-hemmed multitude
detonates;
Shooting off in
firework chaos,
Against the walls
          and each other.
The tunnelled void
                trembles
in the inferno.

When it settles,
The Watchers gather
round their instruments,
Waiting to see
if the blasted millions
had made a spark.

Nathan Ashby

Change

Past these times,
Stuck in way,
Change will come?
Not this day,

They moved ahead,
But you stayed back,
Creeping from the now?
Like you're covered by a sack,

Here you are,
Each new day you say,
The same tomorrow?
Is today,

You should move,
The rest are gone,
You should catch up?
Or forever be one,

Future is tortoise,
Archaic is hare,
One will beat the other?
Until you're there

Nathan Ashby

Face-Papier-Mâché

One look, a single glance,
Enough for my mind to prance,
Faces collide and I don't know
who beside I reside,

Are you Tom?
Are you John?
Am I wrong?

Hurricane in my head,
Identification got no thread,
Forgetting those who I know
I know,

Are you Janey?
Are you Laney?
Am I gone?

First time; it's the last time,
Understanding has become sublime
and I don't know why I'm here,
or you?

Are you Dani?
Are you Rani?
Am I wrong?

Collision of people now,
It's *papier-mâché*, how?
Do you know
Me?

Do I know you?
My thoughts have become blue

Ann Berry

The Last Assault

It was hot and damp and Tolly and his father sat jammed between Xander and Leo with barely room to scratch; four of thirty elite, hand-picked soldiers, tight-packed into a space for half their number, leaning against each other and sweating in silence for what had seemed like hours. Tense, but battle-ready, they sat, heavy-helmeted, in full body armour. Cutting edge weaponry stood between each man's legs ready to grab when the time came to make the drop into enemy territory. Not a word, not a shuffle of feet, not a creak of equipment. How much longer? How much longer? With nerves on edge, faces creased with strain, some breathed heavily, some stared ahead glassy-eyed, some said silent prayers, all old before their time.

Tolly was tired, hungry, dispirited and his leg still ached from last year's wound. He took a sip from the water bottle silently handed round and, as the light faded, leaned against Leo and closed his eyes. He'd left home long years ago, his mother proud that he was going to fight alongside his father for the honour of his country. He'd been enthusiastic and excited at first, racing out of camp with the rapid response team as it moved across the desert plains, seeking out and striking the enemy. The blood-lust had been high; he'd exulted with his comrades over every kill and fallen silent when one of their own was killed. Now, after years of stalemate and no gain, he just wanted to get it over with. One last blood-filled assault and he would be home, either dead or greeting his mother as a war hero like his father.

Falling into sleep he thought he heard women calling, his mother, his sister, Xander's wife, Leo's girlfriend. He shifted, started to speak, and woke with a start to his father's hand across his mouth.

It was completely dark now and his father nudged him to take and eat a handful of nuts and dried fruit. He was still chewing when suddenly there were loud voices outside and they were moving. The men grinned, nodded at each other and stuck up their thumbs.

Action at last. A rumble became a roar. A violent shaking tumbled men into a heap on the floor, the rattling wheels drowning out the sound. After a while they stopped, more shouts, a loud bang, then the voices receded and once more there was silence.

Tolly clutched his father's arm and felt his strong hand envelop his own. In the blackness Xander and Leo's bright eyes and his father's warm touch strengthened him for what lay ahead. At a signal the men quietly moved back from the centre and waited. It seemed a lifetime before there were coded knocks on the outside and Tolly's father, the Company Commander, lifted the trapdoor and flung out four heavy coils of rope. Quickly and silently, soldiers swarmed down hand-over-hand into the night. By the time Neoptolemus and his father, Achilles, dropped to the ground, the gates had been opened and the Achaean Army was pouring into Troy.

Ann Berry

To Hell and Back — Lily 1918

The siren-song warning drew us from our homes and,
  pushing through the crowds with skyward-eyes,
I descended, seeking safety in the Underworld;
the sooty Stygian darkness of the Central line.

Now a white-faced boy lies silent, looks at his missing leg
 while mother, sobbing, cries to heaven for help.
Around the dead and dying, grey-powdered shapes,
bewilderment, bricks and coughing fill the space.

They're carrying the bodies out while blood
  drips down the tiles. And gore-specked blankets,
   toys and body parts lie scattered on the track.
The blood of Bethnal Green flows down the line.

A stabbing pain, a red-wet hand, a three-year widow,
  I am happy dying from the Gotha bomber raid.

Did my Freddie die like this, at a bomber's hand?
  I'll hurry Death to meet him.
    'Here I am, your Lily.'

 At last the darkness grew upon me and

            I saw, in fields of asphodel, yellow-glowing
  upward as if the sun reversed its shine, my Freddie, in
  Welsh wool Sunday coat.
                He waved.
  And as I ran to him, the long and swaying blossom
  brushed bright pollen on the air.

  My heart at heaven's gate, still I wept to see his face.
  His shimmering wraith embraced me and I, sobbing on
  his chest, found solace in the
  cold hard sharpness of his medals pinned. I heard,
      'Come meet my chums from
                Flanders Field'.
  And as I looked, stretched to the horizon through the

pollen-haze, came serried ranks of uniformed and
stumbling dead, all arms outstretched, all unclaimed, all
clamouring to be recognised and loved again.
        Each sought with piteous cries
                a mother, wife, sister, lover, child.

Those Killed in Action, those Shot at
Dawn, those Blinded, Maimed, those Mutilated, those
Prisoners of War, those Grown Old and Died in Bed.

A horde of ghosts early torn from life
        or cursed to live long lives of memory.
All those who'd suffered hell on earth
                and knew this as their home.

    Cowards, villains, murderers.
                Heroes all.

And as they neared I saw they trampled on the
        prone and blistered wraiths of
        black-marketeers, profiteers and Westminster-men
who, blinded, choked and vomited in the yellow-clouded
                    death of mustard gas.

While moustachioed, jodhpur'd generals, swagger-
sticking French and Haig, washed Pilate-hands
                in exculpation.

        'It's not your time'. The words were faint, the visions
fled,
                the arms around me tightened,
                        tugged...

A needle-prick awoke me, a bustling nurse's voice.
    'We nearly lost you, Lily, dear'
I wept to be so cursed.
                Returned to life, a living shade.

A cup of tea? No thank you.
    Freddie's world was heaven
Alone again is Hell.

Karenza Bolton

Sitting for a Portrait

She sat in agony,
He studied her.
His brush,
Inches away from the canvas,
Still untouched.

Her cheeks flushed,
He mixed in more red.

Her hair tickled her neck,
She moved her shoulder
And he flinched in response
Worried his work was ruined.

She could smell him on her nose,
As he studied the angle of the bump,

Becoming suddenly aware
How heavily she was breathing.
Wondering if he was painting
Her breathing in or out.

Blinking became almost difficult,
As he tried to capture the light reflected within.
And she wondered how easily she blinked
Before he ever laid eyes on her.

She watched his fingers flick
With the brush between them.
How gracefully he created
Life from paint she thought

Her own hands stiff and sweaty,
She dared not move them.
He found them too difficult to paint
So did not include them, he told her after.

Karenza Bolton

Somewhere Between

Somewhere between
Asleep and awake,

I find myself drifting,
Waiting, pacing, resisting.

Somewhere between
Dead and alive.

My soul is just twisting,
Changing, chasing, shifting.

Somewhere between
Adolescence and adulthood.

I'm not sure my mind
Ever really understood;

As soon as we are born,
We are dying.

Not for lack
Of trying and lying.

Somewhere between
Okay and crying.
Dying, dying.

But, I'm breathing!
I wake up still breathing!
It's a miracle!

Oh wait, I'm dreaming.
I wake up dying,
Dying, dying.

Roseanne Ganley

The Lighthouse

The waves crashed violently against the white, chalk-lined structure, left unmanned, uninhabited and far from civilisation. A wild, lonely place clawing out of the Atlantic Ocean. There it was, towering high above the island; the lighthouse.

A narrow pathway supported by iron railings sloped up to the lighthouse, a grand spectacle, harbouring its own secrets. Three men docked the island and made their way up towards it, dressed in sea boots and oilskin jackets. Mist covered the tops of the crane platform, used to hoist up heavy goods and equipment, and the ruins of a small chapel outbuilding nestled on the grassy bank.

As the three men approached the lighthouse, they glanced in the direction of the 140,000 candlepower lamp, which stood 275 feet above sea level. A towering beacon of light, erected on the highest point of the island. The three men entered their accommodation and stood at the foot of the tower, which contained bedrooms, a kitchen, a storeroom and a living area. For three days and three nights, this would be their home.

During the first days, they shared old folk stories of 'The Seven Hunters', a group of islands in the North Atlantic known to be haunted. They laughed and drank whiskey, they surveyed the lighthouse and walked around the perimeter of the island several times, which was no longer than a mile in length. On the first day, one of the men had noticed the lifebuoy had been torn from its moorings and fallen onto the concrete path below. The wind had been steady, yet the structure had collapsed unannounced. That night the wind howled, suggesting a storm was on its way. The three men gathered to shelter around the fireplace in the main building and spoke of the voices they had heard coming from the radio earlier in the day.

The first had been calling out for help, one said.
The second had been asking many questions about God, said the other.
The third had been enquiring about the weather, said the last.

On the morning of 15 December, 1960, a severe storm sent a sudden torrent of sea water tearing up the cliff face. One of the men was overcome by the harrowing sensation of nothingness. He ran outside to make sure the lamp was still alight, but found only darkness. Hurrying back to raise the alarm, he found that the other two men had disappeared, their meals left untouched on the table and their jackets and coats still perched on the hook behind the door. The man battled the storm a second time to search for the men, but the harrowing winds guided him as far as the chapel. As he nestled inside, the door slammed against the rocky structure. He fled out onto the edge of the grassy bank to see a bright, green light flashing in the distance. He raced towards it and the darkness consumed him. After his third and final stride, his body plummeted over the edge and was swept away by the Atlantic sea.

The sun rose and all the clocks in the lighthouse had stopped. The craggy rock showed no signs of life. The sea was eerily calm.

Sam 'Jesta' Geden

Allurewrecksinthe

Allure wrecks in the body:
jaded joints and rusted screws,
The wire rot and acid leaks
stinging worn stickers and
razor contours undercover.

The red tape of the beige paper
clumsily wrapped and stretched and sagged,
Surprising no-one who knows
what it took to earn this prize.

Sam 'Jesta' Geden

But I Couldn't Comment

The children don't know
why there are screams,
They called for the two that they trusted.

The fathers are thrashing
and romancing fright —
And the mothers are blinding
and rewinding light —
but I couldn't comment.

So the children learn silence
in the only safe,
Locked up away,
All their fears fear escape —
but I couldn't comment.

The rockstar is lost
in the world's dreams,
Innuendo of life extinguished.

The liars are smiling
and bribing the press —
And the good men are dying
and denied of their rest —
but I couldn't comment.

So the rockstar stays blinded
in breathless space,
Floating away
in a cracked mirror case —
but I couldn't comment.

The man turned up late
to the next day,
Everyone there was already dead.

And the ties are hanging
and banging their sides —
but I couldn't comment.

And police are raining
and trailing the tides —
but I couldn't comment.

And the man tried to breathe
through the tidal waves,
And the homeless dead rise
to greet him his grave,
The Moon turned to dust
as the still soon decayed,
I look away
as the grizzly scene plays...

But I couldn't possibly comment.

Sam 'Jesta' Geden

God is Human Too

Flawless greatness is all they perceive,
Sanctimonious is what's underneath,
People dancing to a heavenly tune,
They refuse to see God is human too.

Oh! God is human too.
Oh! God is human too.
Please forgive me if I leave the prayer room.
Oh! God doesn't care about you.

Stop licking all the holier than thou,
He's no more holy than a wayward clown.
He's just another sinner to tell you the truth,
Why won't you believe God is human too?

Oh! God is human too.
Oh! God is human too.
Please forgive me if I leave the prayer room.
Oh! God's been a bastard to you.

He cannot give up all the light from his star,
It keeps on shining no matter how far.
He didn't do this to be a role model to you,
The myth mystifies a man you never knew.

Keep praying on and on,
Keep hymning the same old song,
Don't forgive me for leaving the prayer room.
'cause you know —

Oh! God never cared about you.
Oh! God's been a bastard to you.

Oh! God is human too...

Sam 'Jesta' Geden

Prosopagnosia

"Kaisa Salieri Jesta
  requests the pleasure
    of your company tonight..."

The valet with brunette tied-up hair
took my keys with nervous intrigue
and a soft-spoken tremor.
The cobweb mansion was cockroach lost
in thousands with garish fashion
and kaleidoscopic rot.

  Salieri is a cold man.
  He promised you came but all I saw
  was a sea of countless coat-tail riders
  dressed to hide in bright disguises.
  He was the only one I knew on sight:
  trademark red and black
  vaudeville and battered top hat.
  It sounded like he was smiling
  as he passed and patted my back.
  I felt through alleys
  of great pretenders,
  Sound and style made to fool
    anything I would remember,

Like how back then
you walked by my side until I saw
and said that we met the night before,
I tried to apologise
but you had your hair down now
which actually made you harder to ignore.
You laughed and we went out for food,
You cried when I told you the truth,
But it could never imperfect your pulchritude.
Not you.

Plastic masqueraders absorbing feasts
and making wine disappear like
a magic trick you know but can't perceive.
Plastic masqueraders absorbing feasts
and making wine disappear like
a magic trick you know but can't perceive.
He conducted the silver symphony
to score those silent years devised
when I went to work for Salieri.
I just wanted to find you so we could escape
but every mask looked the same:
Flawless marble on pearl tie pedestals
like every Renaissance painting.

I wearied from his Havisham
to my human dereliction
of grand design and poor execution.
The valet brought my car around,
And in my haste I almost passed
before seeing her tied-up hair now down
and her soft-spoken tremor asked
if I found what I was looking for.

Sam 'Jesta' Geden

The Prison of St. Autistation

My Castle reshaped by my usurper
and ambushed by Warden Asperger,
I'm here again in the Prison
of St. Autistation.

Shoved into cramped familiarity,
Guards threatening every old routine:
Obsession, Stutter and Isolation.

The corner strips me to my childhood,
The shaded bars were once a comfort
to hide from a staring confrontation.

Quiet corrupted from Kafka deaf-cries
made louder still by Pandora's mind,
The sentence starts in the Prison
of St. Autistation.

Obsession paints the bloated rotting thought
once more on the grey and wrinkled floor,
Reframing away all deviation.

The words I write on the wall make no sense,
Stutter next door dysmorphs their defence,
Now salad speaking self-flagellation.

Canine corpses laugh as Isolation
makes stray eyes my humiliation,
He invites them in the Prison
of St. Autistation.

The new framework breathes like an open tomb
but the air thins out beyond my room,
No doors needed for my suffocation.

Outside the shaded bars I see
the Steps where the Crew used to meet,
Before the call of Great Expectation.

Stutter discovers Obsession mangled,
Fractured screams and distinct high cackles,
Pregnant shadows in the Prison
of St. Autistation.

Bitter numb confessions learned and rehearsed
made to sign by Warden Asperger,
Charged by the Guards' dying allegation.

These walls hold cold the drawn-out silver night,
Paws echo through the silent confine,
Rooted too deep for any salvation.

Asking my name in diseased nostalgia,
Banter-cackling revived Hyenas
corner me hoping for Dawn's invasion…

Golden Day purges the Prison
of St. Autistation.

Ezgi Gürhan

Phaedra

The unfortunate
Victim of the deities.

Miserable woman
In love.

Your passion, your doom.
Your husband, your prison.

Your destiny;
Your greatest enemy

Your love for Hippolytus,
Never a possibility.

His heart never yours,
But Aricia's.

And with your lies he expires
With *her* name on his lips.

What are you to do now,
Oh, unfortunate Phaedra.

Go pull that dagger,
Plunge it into your sinful heart.

Thus, the Gods have won.
First, Pasiphae
Now, Phaedra.

Both destroyed
By unnatural
Passion and desire.

Ezgi Gürhan

Ariadne

Down into the labyrinth
Theseus goes with your
Thread and sword in hand.
He slays the beast
Grabs the glory,
Yet your name is nowhere to be.
He steals you away
To the shores of Naxos
Only to leave you be.
You believed his lies
I'll be back he said
And you waited for him
Your wit made his glory

Was this how he would treat you?
What he had promised you?
To abandon you in these unknown lands
With no love or future!
For no other than your own sister!
Do not let their treachery
Go unpunished,
Oh, unfortunate victim of
a world made for men!

Rise up!
Move forth!
Do not let their frail minds
And selfish hearts define you.

Ezgi Gürhan

Cassandra

Raped and defiled
Your home and people,
Raided and slaughtered.

To see calamity
Yet, not a soul to listen.

Taken to foreign lands
By a man who has spilt
His own blood,
Only to be murdered
By his vengeful wife.

You told them
Of Troy's future,
You told him of
His and your deaths.

They didn't listen.
No one ever has.

A high price to pay
For having refused a man
Don't you think?

Ezgi Gürhan

Medusa

He;
The rapist.
You;
The culprit.

She,
A Goddess,
Side by side
With beasts.

They made you,
their prey,
She made you
The monster.

Your beautiful hair,
Taken away,
Now hissing snakes
On your head,
To petrify.

No longer can men
Look you in the eye
They tremble in terror
As they turn to stone.

They fear you so very much
Because they can
Touch and own no more
All they see and want

Oh, Medusa,
Do they fear you
Because your hair
Is no longer tame.

Or because,
They can no longer
Plunder you
And your sisters?

Almighty Goddesses,
Mere playthings
In a world
Made for men.

Too afraid, meek,
And selfish
To defend
Their sisters

For, if they do,
They will lose
Their side
By men.

Your body
Defiled,
Yet still she's
Unsatisfied

She sends
More beasts
For your
Head.

Ezgi Gürhan

Morrigan

Worshipped by many,
Seated in the heavens.
Dethroned by mortals,
Too jealous to have a woman
As an object of devotion.

First, they made you
Morgan le Fay,
Lady of Avalon.
Then sister to a King.
Sorceress,
Mistress of potions and poisons
Until your name was drenched
In mortal sin and lies.
No Longer a goddess,
But a wicked witch,
Envious of all,
Set out to destroy.

Such great lengths
To sully a holy name.
Such injustice
Yet, not a soul to care.
After all,
A wicked witch,
A goddess,
A woman
are all the
same.

Fanny Haushalter

Four Untitled Poems

I looked through the window,
Admiring the colours of fall;

The trees never seemed so lovely,
Warm shades illuminating the sky
All this beauty was painful to see
And it made my heart drop slightly.

I then realized why.
Everything was dying.
And so did my hope.

****

Our atoms were calling to each other:
Black diamonds seeking
The rays of the darkest sun. In the blinding darkness,
We were perfectly wrong together.

****

Castles made of sand
Crumbling under reality;
Glancing back at how proudly
The marble stood in the past.

Was it even real?
Is my brain sweeping off the dust?
Painting it gold and turning it into
The sweetest golden cage
Just to keep my heart safe?

****

They accused him of madness
Painting the skies coral blue;
Amber flowers in lilac haze;

Flaming poppies in the greenest field.
But he saw the beauty in contrast,

He put life in art
And lost his own.

Harry Hughes

A Walk in Saint Paul's Cathedral

Enter, amazed
For you cannot not be:
The artistry of men
Is paramount.

It lives within the halls
And the domed ceiling
In the wood,
In the gold and in the plaster.

This is where God should be
At least,
So I am told.

I see no god,
I hear no god.
I see and hear men and women,
Who paid to visit the wonder of dead men.

Who venture beneath, to Shit
And to purchase Tat of old London
As they walk over carpeted gravestones.

Sophie Jeans

The Man who Tried to Stop the Tides

There
once was
a man who
wanted to
stop
the tides
after the ocean
had claimed his wife
and drew her out to
lie with it forever
and it left
him all
alone
and so
he tried to
find a way to
stop the tides once and
for all since now all remained
were the pieces of his broken heart.
on the first day he tried
to build a fence around
the sea but he
ran out of
wood at
dusk
and so
on the second
day he tried to
capture the moon and pull
it down to shore where he
could keep it forever in his wife's
jewellery box and keep it by his bed
for without the moon, there can be no tides.
he sat on the beach and wove a
rope out of seaweed until it stretched
the length of the island and
back but no matter how

hard he tried he
still could not
capture the
moon
and so
on the third
day he went to
the town to hire a
team of fifty of the strongest
men each he would pay a fine
sum if they would wade out to the
bay with him and push back the tide for
if it is strong enough to take his wife from
his arms then surely fifty of the strongest men can push
with theirs and stop the tides and so they stood
in line and they pushed back against the currents
all day and all night until their arms
were weak and their legs gave up
soon the man was all alone
until he too was taken
by the tide and
reunited with his
wife at
last

Daniel C. Jeffreys

A Chicken that Shares Our Values

I knew something was wrong when I spent ages staring at poultry in Waitrose. I kept rereading the advert: *'a chicken that shares our values,'* and thinking, does that chicken *really* believe in a free market, democracy, in being organically grown and then butchered? Butchered, what's more, without the benefit of private health insurance.

No one else was bothered. The guy behind the meat counter went on wrapping steaks, a woman with dyed orange hair glided past with that overwhelming whiff of entitlement. "A chicken that shares our values" was clearly unremarkable, but I was gripped.

When I woke up on the Avondale Ward a fortnight later, I thought that the symbols might have come to an end. They shook their quicksilver chains and I followed. They drove me up scaffolding at night to puzzle over obscure blue plaques. I didn't dare miss a single bulletin from any one of these dead artists. In all the confusion, they might offer a clue. Whether I should become a collector, a watercolorist, a diarist or failing all that just a lover of the arts like the plaque outside the old Kensington Spa with its list of artistic types in order of decreasing importance.

I'd always played it safe. I read the ingredients on jars of pickle, was careful with my E numbers. I checked the side effects on bottles of medication — the sleeping tablets that gave you wonderfully gory nightmares (my secret reason for taking zopiclone). I stopped at roadsides, waiting for the green man, walked further than I needed to or turned right if a filter light blinked on, thinking the symbols in themselves might carry me to other places. Even to the thing itself.

But then I worried about the fragility of road signs. One stormy night I watched the street signs buckle with light in the wind: here was our tiny demarcated area of life and sex and social housing and above was the swirling sky and thick black cloud. We might have been settlers, lunar colonists trying to regulate the irregularities of our time-wasting lives. The wind could destroy our chimneys and satellite dishes and our tiny temporary settlement.

The invisible boundaries that held the signs in place were inherently unstable. It was enforced by convention and good will. I tested people's patience. I bought a joke bread roll that squeaked like a seagull and played with it for over two hours on the circle line crying with laughter.

Driving back from Suffolk I saw a huge juggernaut carrying sheep. It had crashed and was sprawling through the central reservation, the buckled metal harnessing the monster, the head — half hanging in our world of oncoming traffic — with lights ablaze. Sheep were huddled along the metal rail, shapeless sacks used to shore up houses against floods. And weeks later I read the driver had reached into his glove compartment to unwrap a cough sweet.

Exhausted, I painted a zebra crossing on my bedroom floor (it had more protective power than a pentagram) and then lay on it to sleep. But when I shut my eyes, I heard engines revving, spoiler exhausts, accelerating mopeds. I believed I was marooned on a traffic island somewhere off the A40.

My sister was bending over me, 'Why, Daniel... you promised me last time... you were going to stop all this...'

'Just a virus,' I said. I didn't like the concern in her startled eyes or the key chain dangling from her bag, a studded sputnik for interstellar communication or a mace from a medieval tourney or something like something else...I had to stop.

The nurse was looking over, the one who called me Jeffrey and told me that 'I would never die.' I had horrible thoughts about all the red resurrected dead, climbing through the earth with sinews popping. What was spoken became an image behind my eyes, swelling and tilting until there was no blackness, just things sliding past on a conveyor belt.

'Look, it's up to you if you want to get out play their game. Stop talking such crazy stuff,' and then she noticed the swelling under my eye, 'How did that happen?'

'I touched a woman doctor's nose,' I said, 'and then a man came out of the wall.' She was getting angry, but I was already slipping under the ocean, the therapeutic sea, flapping past sharks and big business tycoons and pills, great effervescing pills sinking into the depths with their trail of silver bubbles.

I wanted to get well but I doubted there was anything within, nothing to renew all the black, exhausted earth and the fear in my legs and stomach. When Dr. Bozovich talked of renewal, I kept thinking of a crocus in a woodland glade and how long it would take for me to throw up one solitary shoot. "Step into the light." I kept repeating, chewing my bloodied lips — just the right sunbeam and a shot of vitamin D and my brain chemistry would fizz with bearable excitement. 'Step into the light,' I said and then it was lights out all over again.

Jennifer Li

Charlotte's Call

They were sitting in his office. The walls were a blend of white and glass, as if trying to create an illusion of space despite the lack of size. A white gloss desk separated Charlotte and the suited man. Behind him was a shelf of glass trophies and photographs with people that she recognised from the movies. A large window to the left revealed the sunlit Californian cityscape, a crowd of skyscrapers shimmering in the light, undoubtedly containing similar-looking offices with white walls and fake plants.

The man held the picture. His arm was outstretched, as if he were an artist measuring proportions with a pencil. Then his eyes flicked between her and the photo.

'Are you okay? You look tired,' he said.

He placed the photograph back onto his desk. It was the headshot she sent in.

Charlotte's face went grey like the monochrome print.

'Yes,' she said. 'I'm just not wearing makeup.'

A wince contorted the man's face, followed by an awkward chuckle that displayed his perfectly white teeth. He held his hand up.

'My mistake, my mistake.' He exhaled — looked at the photo again. 'Man, you forget what a difference makeup makes.'

He gave another half-chuckle. She did not laugh. He put the print down.

'Anyway,' the man said, 'That does lead me onto what I needed to speak to you about.'

His watch was silver, Charlotte noticed. She focused on it to control her breathing.

'Are you happy with your career?'

She thought about the amount of auditions she went in for and never heard back from. She thought about her few minor roles and the latest one where the scene was cut; about her waitressing jobs and struggling to make enough tips to make rent, her family wanting her to work in their convenience store back home. His watch was a Rolex. There were crystals where the numbers would be.

'It could be better,' she said.

'I agree.'

'You do?'

'Of course,' said the man, and this time his face twisted into what Charlotte supposed was meant to convey sympathy. 'Now, normally at this point, we would reconsider your relationship with the agency.'

Charlotte froze. She could not return home. This was her shot.

'I say *normally*,' the man continued, taking silence to be an adequate response. 'But I think there is another course of action we can take.' He clasped his hands together. 'A change of appearance, perhaps.'

'I—' Charlotte let out a tiny laugh. She could do that. 'You mean a haircut? Different clothes?'

Yet her chest tightened.

'I mean your nose.'

It was as if she was drenched in icy water. All she could do was blink dumbly at him, feeling the remains of her heart pulsate feebly, her mouth devoid of words. She would have felt better had he punched her.

'It's a very common procedure,' the man said.

A part of Charlotte was shocked at the man's audacity; another part sunk with the realisation that this could not be his first time.

'But it can be life-changing. It makes you that much more marketable.' He leant back in his recliner, either unaware of the effect of his words or uncaring. 'It's just the reality of the industry.'

Charlotte forced herself to regain composure.

'But I'm a good actress.'

The man had the gall to laugh.

'You're not the only one. L.A. isn't sorted by good actresses and good-looking people, unfortunately. Many people tick both boxes. This could make your career, Charlotte. But by all means, carry on as you are. After all,' The man pulled out a glossy brochure and slid it in front of her, 'what would I know?'

And he tapped the brochure where it read '25 Years' Experience' under his name.

Twenty-five years of experience. Charlotte barely had one. She had four years of drama school and hardly anything to show for it.

'I need an answer in a week,' the man said.

He could have been talking about a contract deal instead of the anatomy of her face.

'I just — I can't.' Charlotte clenched her fists. 'It's not something I can afford.'

It was true. Even if she could entertain the thought, her income was drained by food and rent.

The man leant over to the side in his recliner chair to open a desk drawer. There were sounds of rummaging, until he resurfaced, victoriously waving a business card. He rose from his chair then walked around the desk to where she sat.

'I have a friend,' he said, passing the card to her. 'One of the best plastic surgeons in L.A. Call him, mention my name—'

'But—'

'And I'm sure something can be worked out.'

He remained where he was, continuing to tower over her. The meeting was over.

Charlotte picked up her handbag from the floor, placed it onto her shoulder, and stood up. Her white chair was hard and positively diminutive compared to his leather recliner. She smoothed down her black dress, holding the card gingerly.

'I'll have a think,' she said, because she could not bring herself to thank him.

'Do.'

The man gave a pearly salesman smile, then offered his hand. She shook it. He had a firm grip.

Charlotte's smile was more of a grimace. She turned and walked away, past the fake plants and the chrome-framed certificates on the wall. Each step felt heavy.

'Charlotte?' he called, when she was at the doorway.

She jerked her head around.

'I'm giving you a chance here.'

Charlotte forced a curt nod. She stepped out of his office, still holding the business card.

****

Charlotte stared at her phone screen, waiting. Between its mild cracks, the loading screen for the video call peered back at her, showing the front camera's view. She saw herself: all brown eyes, brown hair, full eyebrows. Olive skin. Big nose.

Charlotte knew her nose was on the large side. It had a bump too, a source of self-consciousness exacerbated since arriving in Los Angeles one year ago. No one mentioned it though. When prompted, her mother had told her that she was beautiful, and it gave her character.

Perhaps she had been lying. Perhaps everyone had been lying by omission.

The business card was next to her on the grey futon.

'Lottie!'

Instead of her parents' faces, Charlotte was greeted with a shaky view of their compact kitchen. She could make out the black tiled floor, the walnut cupboards, the matching countertop. It was relatively cluttered — most of the space was taken by the toaster, bread tin, and various sauces. It looked exactly as it did when she left, except that the cactus on the windowsill had grown flowers.

Charlotte glanced around her white-walled apartment. There were no flowers here. It was almost bare as the day she moved in, save for the futon, and the collapsible black table and chairs.

'Oh, hold on—' her father's voice was saying.

'There we go!'

Her parents' beaming faces popped up on the screen: her mother with the same brown eyes, her father with the same full eyebrows, and a thick grey moustache. They were waving at her. The camera was very close to their faces, as though they were trying to get the best look at their daughter.

'Hi, Mum. Hi, Dad.'

She waved back.

'We miss you, darling,' Mum said, while Dad nodded profusely.

'I miss you guys, too,' Charlotte replied.

Los Angeles had a lot of things, but it lacked her father's food and her mother's hugs. It felt different coming home to an empty apartment.

'How's your day been, then?'

'Oh, you know,' Dad said, smiling. 'Just sorting out stock and things for the shop. Nothing interesting.'

'We've had more work since you left, Lottie!'

'Is that so?'

'Yes, the shop's busier,' Mum explained. 'We think it's because Susan set up a Facebook page for us—'

'Which is great, since I've got no-one to help me count up all the stock now.'

'That's ridiculous, *I* help you count up the stock…'

As her mother resumed talking about Susan and her technological prowess, Charlotte grinned. This was home.

'Anyway,' Mum said, putting a hand on Dad's shoulder, 'what's most important is how you're doing.'

'Definitely.'

They gazed at her in anticipation: her mother leaning forward, her father with raised eyebrows. They looked remarkably like they did last year, when Charlotte told them she had news to break. Then she had declared her desire to move to Los Angeles to pursue acting.

Charlotte opened and closed her mouth. What could she say? What would they think? Her eyes fell onto the surgery clinic card next to her. The white stood out against the grey of the futon. Its dandelion logo evoked nature.

'Lottie?' Her mother sounded concerned.

Charlotte bit her lip.

'What would you thin—' She tore her eyes away from their faces and drew a deep breath. 'How would you feel if I got a nose job?'

'What?' Mum exclaimed, while Dad spluttered incoherently. 'Why?'

'I just...' Charlotte looked back at the screen then regretted it. Both were gaping at her in disbelief. 'Maybe it would help my career.'

'Don't be silly,' her father said.

'But you're already beautiful, why would you think that?'

Charlotte looked down.

'I don't know,' she lied. 'Lots of people get surgery. I guess you need to look good to get onto the screen.'

'But you do look good,' her mother said. 'You look beautiful.'

The agent would not agree.

'Everyone looks beautiful here,' Charlotte responded. 'Everyone is prettier.'

She gazed at them, imploring them to understand. Everyone in Los Angeles seemed to be slim, but with fat in the right places. They had perfect eyes, lips, noses. She did not have that.

'Maybe it's what I have to do. It's the reality of the industry,' she said, quoting the man.

Her parents shared a look. Then they nodded simultaneously.

'We're coming to get you,' Mum said.

'You can work in the shop.'

It was like Charlotte's stomach dropped off a cliff. All that time in drama school spent pursuing her ambition, only to end up taking over a shop that she hated working in — that was her future if she went back.

'No.'

'You did not go to four years of drama school to get a nose job,' her father said.

'Look, it's not for certain—'

'I should hope not, surgery is a big thing—'

'You said you would support me,' Charlotte pointed out. Her heart was beating fast. 'You said no matter what.'

'We did.'

On the upper right corner of her screen, the phone clock read 4.53pm. The card stated the clinic would close at five.

'I have to go,' Charlotte said.

'What—?'

'I have dinner.'

'We need to talk,' her father protested.

'I need to—'

'Lottie,' Mum said.

Something in her voice gave Charlotte pause.

'Promise me you will really think about this.'

She scanned her parents' faces. They looked much older than they did when the video call began, happily waving to their daughter from the kitchen. She felt her heart tear.

'I promise.'

'Attagirl.' Her mother exhaled in relief.

'We will talk about this later,' said Dad.

There was no room for discussion.

'Yeah,' Charlotte said quietly. 'I love you both.'

'We love you too.'

'Lottie,' Mum said, just as Charlotte went to tap the 'end call' button, 'You really are my beautiful girl—'

Her parents' faces disappeared with a popping sound as the video call ended. Charlotte was alone in her apartment again, staring at the blank phone screen. Would they think she meant to cut her mother off?

It was 4.54pm now.

She could call them back, but she would be unable to make an appointment with the clinic. Considering how the man had given her one week to decide, she needed all the time and information she could get. Acting was her dream. Drama school had solidified that; nothing could match the exhilaration of being in a scene. When the agency first contacted her five months ago, she was ecstatic. This was what she had worked for.

Perhaps her nose did not require changing. Barbra Streisand had kept her original nose and she definitely succeeded. But that was decades ago. She thought back to the man's office, to the photographs of him posing with movie stars. Perhaps he was right. Streisand was not the norm.

The man would say it was the reality of the industry.

Charlotte went to unlock her phone—

The lock screen was her with her parents in front of the Hollywood sign. The photo was taken years before her move to Los Angeles. She usually focused on the sign, however now, she scrutinised the bright smiles on her parents' faces. It was her suggestion to visit the sign in the first place. They had trekked for hours without a single complaint, simply happy to support her. Her father was right. Surgery was a big thing.

'You really are my beautiful girl,' her mother had said.

Perhaps home would be good for her. But acting was her dream.

Charlotte picked up the phone, ready to call.

Petra McQueen

The Cellar and the Attic

The building shattered. Darkness then light. Roof splitting, front wall blown clean away. As the Afghan sun glittered through powdered concrete, there was a smell of cordite and a hideous silence. Slowly, unsure if the movement would hurt, Charlie lifted his head and found Dylan next to him, clutching the top of his arm, blood oozing over his fingers.

Charlie turned his head from the sight and used Dylan's shoulder to stand. 'Boys?' he called. 'Boys?'

A ringing silence. No groans, no cries. Only rubble and a boot with what looked like a pink sock poking out of it. A backpack dangled from a ledge, swinging like a hanged man. Charlie squinted past the jagged remains of the front wall. Some poor woman was pulling her torso along the road, legs so crushed she dragged a trail of red. He saw her only for a moment, long enough to burn her into his memory, then his attention snapped up and beyond her. A Jeep danced over the scrubby hill opposite: crowded with men.

He turned to Dylan. 'Get up!' But Dylan was keening some Welsh prayer. 'Come on!' Charlie pushed at his back, trying to lift him.

The sound of the Jeep came clearer. Charlie would have to leave Dylan. A lifetime's friendship, three years serving together, and he'd have to leave him. He searched for a place to hide.

In the corner, a slab of concrete was propped against a solid wall. He abandoned Dylan and ran over the rubble, blocking the thought that beneath his feet were his men. Even before he tried to slip behind the slab, he realised it was no good. Dylan, compact and wiry, could've done it, but not he. He charged back, searching for someplace else. As he did so, the sound of his footsteps changed.

He swept debris from the floor. There was a trapdoor with a small hole in it to hook a finger round. One sharp wrench and cool, dank air rose from the square of black.

Dylan groaned. 'Take me with you.'

Charlie hesitated: Dylan would slow him down. He was tired of command, of always being the one in charge. Immediately, he was ashamed: he was a protector, not a coward. Using his body as a brace, he dragged Dylan down the narrow wooden steps. The cellar was tiny and filled with boxes. From the pictures on the packaging, the boxes must have once been stock for a toy shop above. He lowered Dylan, ran back up the ladder, and closed the trapdoor. In his mind's eye, he saw the clear space and trail of his own footprints above them.

Aside from a rim of thin light around the door, it was as black as his father's attic. There was the same thick scent of dust and dank; the same panic that the objects were alive and could leap out. Sick with fear, Charlie reached for his rucksack to get out his torch, but the pack had gone. The one he'd seen dangling from the shard of concrete must have been his. At once, Charlie understood that he'd been blown backwards in the blast. He touched the back of his head and found it was wet.

'Dylan. Get your torch.'

Dylan made no sound.

In the nightmare dark, Charlie groped his way to Dylan, found his torch and switched it on. Dylan was deathly pale. As he toppled forward, Charlie caught him and felt the damp of Dylan's blood. 'Hello, lad,' Dylan slurred over Charlie's shoulder. He muttered something in Welsh, then switched to English. 'Been here before, ain't we, boy? Remember, remember the fifth of November.'

His head slumped. Charlie lowered him to the floor, resting him against a crate.

'Dylan!' Charlie shook him. 'Dylan!' Even as he slapped his face, he knew it was no good. Dylan was dead; and, although he waited for it, the sorrow Charlie wanted to feel wouldn't come. There was no pain: only a dry emptiness.

It was only when he lay Dylan down and sat next to him, the thoughts came: if only he hadn't led the men into this deserted shop; if only there wasn't this godforsaken war; if only Dylan had ignored him when Charlie had pressed him to join up. He fingered the back of his head and allowed himself to think he too had died and had nothing left to be ashamed of.

A rat scuttled across the floor to the far end of the room. Charlie shone the light in the rat's wake. And there, crouched on top of a box, feet tucked up, arms holding knees, was a little boy.

As Charlie jumped, the beam danced. The boy's shadow was a monster and then gone. Charlie stood and inched towards him, blinking hard to focus. The boy was so grimy it was difficult to make out his features but he seemed familiar. Perhaps he was one of the kids who hung round the perimeter of the base until their parents dragged them off, cuffing their heads.

'Assalamu alaykum,' Charlie whispered to him in faltering Pashto. Spotting he was wearing Superman pyjamas, Charlie pointed at his chest and lifted his arm in the hero's pose. The boy pulled a toy fire-engine out from the hollow between his knees, clutched it, and lifted his head towards the trapdoor.

Charlie froze. The kid could have brothers up there, his father, an uncle. Any moment, he would scream out. An image flashed of suffocating the boy:

quickly, quietly, to kill the problem. He took a step towards him.

Sounds of gunshots thundered above, and Charlie's attention was wrenched to his men: Jacob Freegazer; Big Micky Patel; Sam Johnstone; Acne Andy. All gone. He looked across to Dylan. Dead too.

Above, the square of light wavered. Footsteps sounded above his head. The boy looked up towards the trapdoor, face grim with determination, clutching his fire engine. Was there enough time to silence him? As he took a step towards him a machine gun hammered a burst of rounds against the trap door.

TAT-TAT-TAT-TAT-TAT.

The wood shattered. Fingers poked through the holes and the trapdoor opened. Unable to move, a stream of piss ran down his leg. Charlie watched as a head, wrapped in a black kaffiyeh, hung down into the cellar. Machine gun in hand. Although he couldn't see a gun, Charlie knew he was outnumbered. He Charlie lifted his hands and looked at the kid: *I saved your life, boy. I could've wrung your neck but I let you be. Plead for me.* But it was as though the man could see neither him or the boy. He stared only at Dylan: a fallen hero in a shaft of light. With a quick word to the men above him, the head withdrew. There came a thick boot and another.

The men were in the cellar now. Not one of them had seen Charlie yet, cowering against the boxes, but they would soon. Next to him the boy fidgeted. Charlie put out a steading hand but the boy twitched from him, knelt down, and pushed his fire engine towards the men. As Charlie stopped it with a panicked foot, the boy gave out a high-pitched scream. The men turned and the boy ran towards them, towards Dylan, as they fired. Charlie squeezed his eyes shut.

The boy was dead and Charlie was dead, he knew it. Behind his eyelids was a dark attic: Dylan screaming; fireworks whizzing and snapping. The attic was where it all began; and the cellar where it ended. Yet other things crept through: smell of cordite and death; footsteps; a Jeep starting; the pump of Charlie's heart in his ears; the sound of his breath.

Slowly, Charlie opened his eyes. The cellar was empty. Empty but for Charlie and Dylan and the boy. A boy who couldn't be killed: a boy who somehow, and for some reason, had protected him. Charlie's arms trembled as he crawled to him. 'Thank you.' He couldn't remember the Pashto.

There was such fire in the boy's eyes, that Charlie staggered to his feet. He was afraid of the boy. Afraid too, of the sight of Dylan, who never should've been here.

****

Three months later Charlie was back in Aberystwyth, tramping up Penglais Hill. Slate grey houses, slate sky, monolithic university. At the top was Dylan's house. It was smaller than he remembered. But, he supposed, it had always been small compared to his own father's gothic structure in town.

Dylan's dad let him in and then sat back in his armchair, gut spilling over his lap. He didn't shake Charlie's hand. But then again, he never had. It wasn't so much he hated him, Charlie told himself, just that old Welsh way of despising any English speaker.

Charlie sat on the faux-leather sofa. 'How have you been?'

Dai grunted.

How much easier it'd been at the other soldiers' houses where platitudes came easily. Here he had no status. He was Dylan's dodgy English friend. A poor motherless boy who'd arrived from London at the age of ten and turned Dylan's life upside down. But what would Dylan have been doing if it wasn't for Charlie? Cleaning up after tourists in a two-star hotel? In prison like his uncle? His skin crawled as he remembered what actually had happened.

Charlie looked at Dai, hoping for eye-contact, an opportunity to express his grief. Dai was staring stonily at the television blasting out some a repeat of *Antiques Roadshow*. A woman was beaming, turning a toy car over and over in her hands.

Dylan's mum bustled in.

'Dai! You could've told me Charlie was here.' To Charlie: 'He's a useless lump. Stand up, love. Let's have a look at you.'

Charlie was already on his feet. She took him in her arms. Waft of cheap perfume and bleach. A lump caught in Charlie's throat, and his voice was tight when he spoke. 'I'm sorry for your loss.'

She drew back, lips tight.

Dai said something in Welsh.

'I can hold the boy if I want to,' she said. Charlie was grateful for the English. 'Cup of tea? Oh, sure you do' she said to Charlie, and left as quickly as she'd arrived.

Below the noise of the television, Charlie made out the radio in the kitchen. He imagined Awel bustling about. She'd always been feeding them and he'd always felt more at home here than in the echoing rooms of his father's house. Even when Dylan had said he didn't want to play anymore, he'd come round, just to see Awel. An image flashed of his pinching Dylan's thigh moments after Awel had kissed the boy's head. Dylan's eyes had watered, but he'd said nothing.

He tried to block out thoughts by watching the television but could make no sense of the words. Then, with relief, came the sound of the doorbell.

Dai raised his eyebrows. 'Awel! Awel! Deaf as a post she is. Awel!'

'Do you want me to go?'

Dai shook his head and levered himself out of his armchair. Charlie turned the television down. He heard voices: Dai's and a softer one. Sandy! Dylan's older sister. For the longest while, Charlie had had a crush on her. He wiped his palms on his trousers. And stood.

She came in.

'Charlie!' Her smile didn't reach her eyes. How he must remind her of Dylan. She sat so close to him on the sofa, he had to glide his eyes away from her cleavage. They talked about the weather, how much leave he had. He smiled and nodded, but all the while he couldn't help but think of Dylan in the cellar in Musa Qala, slick with blood and pale with pain.

Awel bustled in with the teacups. Mugs of tea steamed on the tray she held under her bosom. Sandy stood to pull out a nest of occasional tables.

It was then that Charlie saw him.

The little boy.

Charlie leapt off the sofa and backed into the bay window.

The boy stared. Deep brown eyes and Superman outfit.

'What is it, Charlie?' asked Sandy.

Throat closed with fear, Charlie couldn't speak.

Sandy grabbed the boy's hand and pulled him towards her. Nestling between Sandy's legs, the boy didn't take his eyes off Charlie.

'You all right, Charlie, love.' Awel held out her hands.

Charlie wanted to reach out to her, to bury his head in her soft chest, but he couldn't unlock his eyes from the boy's. With a sickening twist of his stomach, he saw what the boy was holding in his hands: a toy fire engine.

'Why are you here?' he hissed.

The adults looked at one another.

'This is Dylan,' said Awel.

Charlie shook so much he collapsed against the windowsill.

'It's *Little* Dylan. Sandy's boy, you know?' Her voice was soft. She advanced upon him, palms open, as though Charlie was a wild, frightened beast.

Legs giving way, he slumped onto the floor. The place on his head where he'd knocked it all those weeks ago, throbbed.

With a great huffing wheeze, Awel sat next to him. 'Is it 'cause he looks so much like our boy? Sometimes it breaks my heart to look at him.'

Charlie raised his head and wiped his face with his sleeve. Awel had blocked his view, but he knew the boy was there, watching.

'Is it the clothes? Just like the ones Big Dylan used to wear, right?'

From the back of the room, Dai spoke, voice thick and gruff. 'Ten years old and the English boy told my son he was a baby for wearing stuff like that.'

Awel held up her hand to shush him. Then with a shake of her head, she folded her hand into a fist and laid it on her heart. 'Those pranks you used to play on him gave him nightmares. That time in the attic... those fire crackers. He'd protect you no matter what you did.' She lowered her head as if ashamed of the words.

Dai came over to her. He said something in Welsh, helped her off the floor and led her out of the room.

The sister kissed the top of the boy's head. 'Shall we find a biscuit?'

The boy broke free and ran to Charlie.

'Did you kill my uncle?'

'Dylan!' said the sister.

The boy held up his fire engine: arms straight, one eye shut. The ladder was pointing towards Charlie, black as the barrel of a gun. Charlie raised his body, inching forward, forward, so that his forehead touched the edge of the ladder. Then he spread out his arms, closed his eyes, and waited.

Adam Neikirk

Leander in the Strand

An excerpt from 'Your Very Own Ecstacy'

Then did the voice of childly wonder ring
Like an inverted bell within the wide
Wood-panell'd halls of Christ's Hospital, for
One day the young Coleridge had been out
Skulking in the streets of London — the Strand,
To be precise; and he was playing at
Leander swimming thro' the Hellespont
To meet his Hero, who for him did wait
By an homefire anointing the far side
Of the great ocean (a fix'd and worthy point
Which he had always felt had been his fate);
And as a child's thoughts will be well full
Of but themselves, and will be by their light,
Interior light, that shining from them shews
Some of their colour (some of it from far),
He could not see the world around him, tho'
To be fair to Sam, it did not see him either;
And it so happen'd that as he was crossing the street
His arms stretch'd out as in a swimmer's pose
Who parts the air like water, and makes for
A distant prospect n'er by London spied,
He bump'd into a gentleman, whose head
Was up within that special stratosphere
Of serious talk and pipesmoke, e'en above
The sounds of hockers calling and the mill
And din of general shouts and mockery
That can be felt 'along the blood' of cities,
Like sonic veins; but from his rarefied
And generally pleasant altitude
The man was rudely shaken, by what look'd
Like a nautic beasty charging for his purse,
Another urchin, set to plague the rich
And disappear within an eyelid's space
Into the network of the underworld:

And so he, quick as lightning, clasp'd around
The child's wrist, and dragg'd him to the fore,
And said, "This child has pick'd my pocket!" Sam
Star'd up at him with faintly glitt'ring eyes,
And a smear of dirt across the bridge of his nose
That made him look the part; and yet, he knew
He was no richer; for he had not thought
To steal from those with plenty, and thus assuage
His pelting hunger-pangs; but his mind's eye
Could stop his stomach with a lovely form.
"'Tis all!" he said, and thought his eyes would burst
Their liquid dams with more than liquid tears.
"What is all?" The man's great grey moustache
Upon his lip curled up its hackles like
A feisty cat, such was his puzzlement;
"You mean to say you'll take no more from me?"
His heart by wisdom's discipline had been
So form'd of late, that at this adult's cry,
He search'd about for some one broken rule
Visibly shatter'd; or thought, he ought to produce
A line of proper syntax, or to state
Some Latin rule grammatical (and that
Done with the proper syntax); yet the man
Became so fluster'd, that he shook the child
Expecting to see coins fall from his pockets
And rain against the ground with golden peeps;
Yet nothing happened. "What do you mean, 'tis all'?"

Sam panted hard; he said amongst the gloom
Of biting premonitions, "I meant to say,
That I have not a penny, sir, and so I say
I must divulge my pennilessness to you
To my own shame! I certes am not faultless;
But that my mind can stop my hunger-pangs
With a lovely form, inscrib'd upon my heart,
From which my will might flow, and make my limbs
Strong to control the sea, and not it me.
For you see — I was just now — just now
I was *in* the sea, crossing the Hellespont,
Fighting the current, winning my way to fair Hero!

And the scene, which, as I have stated, need be
So vivid to me, that it became so *real*
And *plug* my poor stomach, sir! had me blinded
To what you, and men like you, might call 'the real'—
This street, this busy street, this hurrying crowd,
And all the objects that they hurry toward."

Sam sigh'd and heav'd a heavy tear, which fell
Into the street, a single drop of rain
On a bright day, which otherwise was cheer'd
By the sight of London's busy industry:
"Believe me tho' I once in an ill hour
Stole from the larder of Christ's Hospital—
You see my coat; I am a poor orphan—
And had my fill of things forbidden to me—
I am no thief! But that I come from Devon,
From Ottery St. Mary, far away,
And have no family here, and scarce a friend
To visit upon leave-days, I go out skulking
And use my imagination to fill in
All these holes in my life." And here he shew'd
The man, whose face had soften'd its resolve
To bestow punishment, and who had set
The child on the ground in gentleness,
And whose moustache had even calm'd, and now sat straight
In its contentment on his upper lip,
His coat, his charity coat, which was so fill'd
With holes, you might have thought Sam was at war
With his own personal army.

                    The man relented:
"What an amazing child thou art! My God!
I am sure you are destin'd to be a Grecian;
And that you'll before long assume your place
At some great university; or perhaps you will
Become a doctor of divinity,
And explain to learned men, the ways of Him
Who made us all! Well — never you fret, my child;
I have a gift for thee (tho' 'tis not gold),
A ticket, to a lending-library, on King Street;

This ticket allows the bearer to withdraw
Two books a week, each week, provided he
Return them dutifully in the proper state.
It is a kind of trust: not only that you
Will be a bookish person, who loves books,
And cares for them, as they were living things;—
But that you will by reading become wise,
Far wiser than your peers!" And here the man
Lean'd close, as would deliver an aside
For Sam alone — tho' we may hear it too:
"I know, it is fierce, the competition, I mean,
To win a scholarship, and to *go up*
To Oxford or to Cambridge — my own son
Hath struggled manfully to write an essay
On the origins of language to that purpose,
And bless him, he recently left with his degree—
But there are many who simply cannot be
Accommodated, you see; we are, or soon will be
At war again — so you must use this ticket
Like an advance of money, which fain I would
Have made to thee, on *paper*, were your case
Brought before me at home. Yet as it stands
I am a bit overdrawn, and so this must
Suffice for you: I think it will for you—
For you seem like one of those *bookish* types,
Who ought dive deep, as Milton did,
And write an epic poem, or some such thing,
When you have laid up many works in store
To be the lead that thy soul turns to gold!"

With that alchemical flourish, the man seiz'd
The child by one of his fray'd lapels
And push'd the ticket down into his pocket
Where it only peek'd out part; and seem'd to make
A kind of handsome pocket-square. Sam beamed.
"You do me too much honor, sir! For I
Confess I am a most inept student; I barely know
A rule of writing to save my life, and I
Am the dullest poet, and have been fairly call'd
By my superiors, a lesson in wasted time.

Yet I do love to read, and I should like
Very much to read such books as have been bann'd
By the Headmaster Bowyer, at our school,
For being wild, rude, low, or indecent;
And then delight my friends, for I have many,
By reciting them *verbatim*: for you see
Tho' I am dull, and slow, and prone to sloth,
And am a glutton, I can remember whole
Long passages of the abstrusest stuff
Without an error! Anyway, I thank you again!"
Now did he swim his way across the street
Before the man could answer; and like an urchin
Vanish'd into the network of thin ways,
And behind shutter-windows; for he had been
Keen to observe thro' th' avuncular months
The ways of drunken rambling, and became
A right mind for the nearest public house;
'Twas how he knew the way to King Street: there
The grand King's Arms, with her peculiar paint
Of yellow-green, and her squat broken face
Did send the hollow fumes of spirits spill'd
Along the chairs and rafters, and the floor
And insides of the windows, wide like wind.
'Twas not too long, in loitering here, that he
Discover'd the library — it was just
Across from the tavern, and facing on,
Tho' he had never noticed it before;
Which was also odd: for it was a grand shape
Amongst the ramble of that London street
Out of the way, and friendly more to those
Who wanted food, or drink, or conversations
Convivial, or to discuss the news,
To lampoon politicians, and mock th' art,
Or science of happiness, call'd politics;
The library was tall, cathedral-like,
Made of white stone, and its two frontward towers
Had domes of burnished gold; it had a look
Almost exotic, and Sam was put in mind,
Where at the front, two great lions of stone
Were frozen in a watchful contemplation,

And the front entrance was a door of other shape
Than he was used, and here and there, a great
Wide-leaved plant hung in the afternoon air
Luxurious, of the *One Thousand Nights*;
As if this were the abode of Scheherazade,
And she its only resident, and all
The books pil'd up, which now he chanc'd to dream
With indeed a bookish relish, were but records
Of all the tales she had told to stay her death.

Robert Newman

Darkness

It was simple logic that in shutting oneself from light, one would forever live in darkness. However, if one refused to see the light, would one know they are in the dark?

His mother once told him it was better to discover day and die, than to live his life in shadows. Now his ears rang with her advice. Each step closer was a daunting task. Burning blood and the rush of adrenaline, his poor heart desperate to beat its way out his chest. He was face to face with the cause of his agony, able to touch the evil that shunned his frail frame and barred him from the beauty of day. After a moment's consideration, the timid man made a decision that sealed his fate. He hit his enemy. A crack broke the silence. Unhappy is he who resents the untouchable past. He hit his enemy. A second crack followed. Wretched is he who only remembers pain and sadness. He hit his enemy. A shatter filled the room. Hopeless is he who cannot feel the present. Another punch. Blood decorated his fist. Another punch. His enemy was falling to pieces. Another punch. Victory?

He staggered back into the darkness, panting like a stray hound. *On the cold floor lay the shattered remains of a mirror.*

Cristina del Pozo Huertas

Of a Red Song

Sometimes he doubts whether the war is over. He knows it must have, since no one quite like him has shown up in a long time. It feels rather oblivious not to know if a war — and not your regular war in faraway lands, mind you, but a *civil war*, the war that broke his country — is over. But, well, his mere existence is rather oblivious and his perception is flimsy at the best of times. There are some days when he is aware of where he is and a bit of what is happening, and he can even move around and remember what he sees, but those days are rare. Those days are usually prompted by something other than his conscience.

He mostly stays in one place, the same place since he was killed, chained to the land, and remembers.

He doesn't really like remembering.

But it's the only thing he can do.

It was the beginning of the war when he fell. Not too long after the blue troops first came to the village…though that's not quite true, is it? They were already there, always had been, that's why they won first. When the blue troops arrived, a list of names was produced. By whose hands or mouth he has never known. Their owner probably came here far too late and old for him to recognise them.

As per the contents of that list, blue soldiers came knocking on his family's door. They took him and the oldest of his siblings, along with anyone else who had a red song playing in their chest. They took them out of the village, by the road along the stream, by the property Don Agustín let them use to feed the cattle; made them stand in formation with their eyes blindfolded, and shot them.

That was before the war was called *war* on the radio.

He knows it ended up becoming one, though.

Time might be what eroded the weight of his presence and mind.

The first few years here were more lucid, although he couldn't move at all back then — time might have eroded his link to his tomb as well. There wasn't a need to know what was going on, though. He could almost taste the dry summer during the first couple of months: the sun was unrelenting as it had always been, not a white cloud on the sky, the wheat gleaming golden. He assumed it was extremely hot, as the cicadas wouldn't shut up — and neither would the men in the trenches, although that didn't have too much to do with the heat.

He wasn't that close to the battle, he didn't see it in first person as he knows some other souls who fell there had no other choice but to. Nevertheless, he could see the clouds of dust that rose from where the cannonballs of the *obuses* hit. He could hear the screams and shouts, the commands, the songs whispered during the night. He could feel the land breaking and bleeding as its men and women did.

When there weren't battles, he could hear the crying from the surviving families in the surrounding villages.

He kept a keen ear for his mother's weeping and wept with her.

There isn't as much blood on the land as there was back then, yet he can see the wounds on the trenches, the ditches, and the streets still pulsing. They bleed a bit from time to time, too, and he can see some of the bullet holes getting more infected by the decade.

If the war has ended (which he isn't sure of) the land hasn't yet found its peace.

He finds evidence of the state of the war on the days he weighs enough to see, hear, and move. He travels and he doesn't know how he does it. He neither walks nor floats and never remembers the journey — so who knows? Maybe he imagines the whole thing? Either way, he travels down to the capital. He had never been there when he was alive. He heard after he was killed that the capital had turned into a citadel, the embodiment of hope for the red resistance: borrowed tanks and a banner reading '*No pasarán*' blocking the access of the armies of the blue side.

He resents the fact that he couldn't *see it* back then. It changes every time he goes, but he knows there are no banners or Russian tanks anymore.

Most of the times he visited, it didn't look like there was a war going on in the capital and he would think then that it had ended: no tanks, no propaganda to join the fight, no debris thrown on the streets after a battle. Except the capital always reeked of death. He would smell the odour long before he arrived and, once he got to the city, he would see it — see death — the men and the women, some barely out of their teens, standing incorporeal, so angry that it was difficult to tell they weren't alive. They didn't talk, though, and they looked at him as he passed. That's how he knew. They showed up after him, he realised, and he also realised that they are quite like him; that they have the same song in their hearts. Still, there are vast differences between him and these men and women. But he isn't able to tell what those differences are.

He has no idea who is winning or has won. He has seen the song that most of those who came after him carry — he's seen it, not heard it — they are like the men and women of the capital. The more of them that came along, the more quietly and angrily they did so, their mouths locked and a strong beat of light setting the rhythm of an anthem. And he thinks he has a terrible idea of who's winning.

A lot of people showed up during those first years dead. He was one of the first, so he got to see most of them arrive. And, contrary to what he expected — he was young and idealistic, so he didn't consider the possibility when he was alive — most of them didn't have a hymn in their hearts that was either blue or red.

Most of them had faded: sad rainbow lullabies. In some of them, the red or the blue strikes were brighter than the rest of the colours, but the combination of all of them still won out.

It was hard learning that someone who could sing the red anthem would cast it aside for the rainbow, and he thought of his mother. He remembered the time before the war, when she brought his youngest sister with her so she could witness the first time women voted; when she would teach him of the dignity of those who work the land and the rights they would have to fight for. He thought of how he hadn't seen her around here yet, of how she had three more children and a maimed husband to take care of. Then he understood why someone would choose the rainbow lullaby over the red anthem.

He wouldn't have. But he understands.

The song he never learnt to understand — and doesn't want to — is the blue one. Sometimes he sees them, those with the blue song in their chests, and he feels like spitting at their feet. He would if he could — if he had saliva to spit, or corporeal lips to spit with, or if their feet touched the ground.

He doesn't like travelling to the capital — not exactly — but since it's the only thing he can do except standing on his ditch and remembering, he does it whenever he is able to.

There were times when he *was* able to — he saw, he heard, he moved — and yet the city repelled him. Those were strange years not too long ago. The blue dead souls threw a tantrum for some reason; the blue living *raged*. He heard the red anthem being sung almost every day, but the various voices clashed with different sentiments. Most sang it happily, relieved, and victoriously, but the melody seemed to have been tweaked. Meanwhile, others sang the original anthem as if they were preparing to commit *murder* (that's what he sounded like right before the war, so it's not like he judged).

A new, strong song he didn't think he had heard before appeared too: it was familiar, it was somewhat similar to the song in his chest, but it wasn't in a language he knew and there were feelings in it alien to him. He didn't know what *that* was about.

He wondered if the war had ended then. If his side had won. He thought so for a long time.

And then, for a little while, the land started to bleed like he hadn't seen in a long time.

A victorious clamour echoes today. A grey clamour, not one bit joyful, shouted as if sung with what's left of the red melody. It's stronger in some voices than in others — the resemblance to the original melody — but in all of them it sounds clear enough.

He decides to get closer to that victorious clamour…is the war over? He's not sure. It doesn't seem so. In the notes of the song there is far too much stale hatred and far too little sadness for it to be the end of the war — not that he'd ever lived to the end of one. It's just that's not what he'd expect it to sound like if it was. He wonders what it would sound like if it had ended, or if it already had and he missed it. There was a time when he thought he had heard it end, a while ago, but souls like him *kept coming* and it's not like he could ask someone about it.

He decides to get closer and the clamour leads him to a monument: a huge white basilica built in a valley.

He knows this place. He doesn't like it, the feeling of being here.

A procession in black carries on their shoulders a Yule log as large as a man — the simile comes to his mind before he can stop it — and he watches as they advance towards a helicopter. It's a restrained ceremony. There are only a few of them and they look small amidst the white of the monument, like ants bringing food home…and yet. Yet… He feels a tremor at the solemnity and greatness of the whole act.

His own body and his siblings' and his friends' still rot in a ditch, no tomb in sight.

Enthralled as he is watching the carriers crawling across the platform, it takes him a while to notice that he is not the only one looking. He can barely see them or feel them, but they are here, silently moving along the procession, observing from the edges, or perched on the big Cross. Once he notices them, he cannot ignore their presence. There are hundreds of them, they fill out the whole space, shells of souls with their hollow cheeks and their eyes full of hellfire.

He has heard of them. They were the last great batch to come, the first one from their side that was different from him and those with the same song as him. They had their voice destroyed before it was their lives' turn. No one has seen their song shine in their chests again.

When he tries to look for the procession again, he finds that he can't. The shells fill out his field of vision. A woman with big, dry eyes stands in front of him. Whatever little is left of her hair hangs around her malnourished face; a snarl on her lips as she watches. She notices him staring and grins at him for a second before she turns back to the procession that he can't see anymore.

Spirits can't talk, but there were words in her teeth.

He leaves. The clamour doesn't come from them anyway, or from the afterlife.

What does it mean for the state of the war, that one of the big blue traitors has been unearthed? That the alive sing victory with such bittersweet voices?

What does it mean for his ditch?

During those first years being dead, he used to seethe unceasingly at the blue troops. He cried a lot too.

He thinks it might have been because he didn't believe yet that he was dead and he didn't understand why he couldn't move and had to watch family and friends die on the field.

His younger sister cried with him. The other two — twins, the oldest daughter and the oldest son — only did so when they heard their parents weep.

They were four siblings: four young red idealists.

They had been killed at the same time, by the same men, who had yet to show up.

Not that it would change anything — not that it *did* when it eventually happened — but back then they all wanted to at least glare at them for robbing them of their lives.

It's not too long after his visit to the basilica that he finds himself conscious again. He can barely see or hear. He can move, so he makes for the capital.

He sees red, yellow, and purple. The alive are congregated and chanting. He doesn't really hear what they say, but he feels the fraternity and the worry in their songs: thoughts of the other great city he didn't get to visit before the war crawl into his mind — and then he hears the shouts.

He sees the dust clouds of the *obuses* and the sun beating down onto the trenches. Then he realises that he doesn't see that at all. He sees black armours and young people shielding their faces as they are cornered; he hears the screams — screams that used to reverberate on the battlefield and up the hill from where he was watching — screams in mouths behind black bandanas, metal bars and chairs and rocks and knifes in hands.

He cries, for the first time after he saw his mother again, so many years ago. And wakes again, hovering over his ditch.

He wonders, again, if the war is over.

Jordan Reddington

La Danseur Noble

Pierre swept a *rond de jambe* through what was once a wonderful stage, unswept with time. He was mindful to keep his form, a straight back, so he didn't slip on the dust. When he carried the piece to completion, he began again. And each time he did this to the accompaniment in his head.

The orchestra had evacuated well before he took to Madame's stage for his own performance. She sat, donned in a fur coat to her feet, fit for the winter weather, and watched each move Pierre made as he made it. He spun downstage, lifted an arm.

She pushed up on her cane, out of the vacant audience, and said, 'That's enough for now. Go home and sleep.'

He stood under the proscenium and listened for silence, heaving, wet with sweat. Without Madame, the theatre was lifeless. And whilst he preferred her company, when it was only him he could perform past midnight at a pace he set; only the two of them would see his piece once it was perfect. As her other dancers had left, Pierre was all she had left to pass time. All she could do as she grew frailer was offer advice.

In the morning, she asked, 'Have you slept?'

Pierre told her, 'I thought whilst I had some time, I'd practice.'

'You mustn't spend all of your time in this place.' And she nodded to the door. Obedient Pierre bowed for her, and did as she'd asked.

It wasn't much of a walk between the theatre and Pierre's apartment, only three blocks, and the road was straight, but for the last turn. As time passed, people forgot the brasseries and boutiques; they fled in the night, left them behind. There were tables beside their sullen chairs, buried by half-torn awnings, and some windows were smashed to nothing — some buildings were blown out of the street, their walls and roofs nothing more than mounds of stone and dust across the pavements.

And though his apartment housed his father, the theatre was where he lived, and the walk became so long. Although she wasn't his birthmother, Pierre felt that Madame had made him who he was and hoped to be, more so than his father. As he too became more fragile, it became a chore for Pierre to tend to his disabled father.

That morning, his papa was spread across the carpet, having fallen in the night, with his walking frame beside him, useless.

'Papa, what happened?' He threw his hands in the air. It was the third time he'd fallen because he didn't want to use the frame. Nonetheless, he knelt to help him to his bed. 'Did you use your walking frame?'

'It's not very far, Pierre. I thought that I could make the few steps without it.'

'You mustn't, Papa. You need your frame to walk now.' It wasn't far from where he fell by the fireplace to his father's bedroom, into his old four-poster bed.

'I can't believe how useless I have become, Pierre.' His father began to weep into his hands, softened by age, 'What's become of me?'

When he saw the old man cry, Pierre sat until he fell asleep; he pitied his papa, and hoped he would not become like him when he was as old.

Because the phonograph only played his accompaniment for so long, there were long periods of silence as Pierre performed. Between his *pliés*, he caught glimpses in the mirror of the man he wanted to be: a ballet dancer, one of the best to command a stage. By far the best in the city. And as it wound into silence, he felt the need to slow, but pranced into *pirouettes* instead. His neighbours could have watched him from their apartments if the windows hadn't been covered to protect him and his papa from the overwatch.

He stopped as his lungs were heavy. They ached for air, and made him stop to breathe — and to listen to the sound of blood as it rushed to his ears, to his head. When it cleared, he heard, without his accompaniment, Madame in the lounge with his father.

'I fear he may be harmed.'

Madame said, 'Have you not seen him shoeless? With how much he spins, his toes are almost worn to nothing.'

'What can be done, then? I don't want him to become like us.'

'Have you not seen? We have to evacuate by next week. The theatre is unreachable, so he'll soon see there's nothing left here.'

'And if he doesn't leave? What am I to do then? I worry for him so much, Madame.'

'As do I, but you must also ask yourself: what would become of you should something happen to him?' asked Madame.

'He would not allow such a thing to happen.'

Madame moved to the door, her feet almost silent on the stained carpet, and left the old man in his chair by the mantel. So that he could not be called for, Pierre poured his accompaniment from the horn of his phonograph, superseding the sound of mortar shells totalling the many boulevards previously untouched.

He stretched *en pointe*, spread his arms out and withdrew into himself, *pirouetted* and pranced upstage. Pierre hadn't noticed her as she stepped in, but when he lifted his posture to finish, she saw how he'd spent his efforts. It had rewarded him well, as he stood in place, perfect form, panting.

'Why are you here?' Her theatre was soundless, so her voice filled all of it.

'Why wouldn't I be here?' He bowed for Madame, 'I have to have my performance perfect for opening night, don't I? Am I to leave our audience without a performance to watch?' He sat on the edge of the stage, cross-legged.

'Why would you be? I will not be here by tomorrow morning, and I recommend that you flee as well, Pierre. It is not safe here anymore,' she said, and she looked over her shoulder at the theatre entrance, eaten away by artillery fire.

He frowned, asked: 'Should I practice more? I'm sure that I can make t perfect, perhaps if I practice tonight.'

'I'm sorry, Pierre. I must leave. I hope that you and your papa will do the same.' And there she left him.

She was stretching him thin, asking if he was willing to persist to achieve the perfection she sought. So, he thought it best he not waste another minute, and continued, 'I'll have it perfect, Madame! Don't worry! It'll be perfect!'

When he did not spend his days at the theatre, he spent them in his small studio, where he once slept. He used his phonograph for the accompaniment, and had a mirrored wall so that he could make sure he kept his perfect form. His door was shut, so that his father would not interrupt with his wittering. Pierre had to have it complete by opening night.

With so many eyes, how was Madame to refute his commitment? He would become her best. He would be at the top. In his mirror, he liked what he saw. His stature was that of a professional performer, straight-backed, tall, proud, like he owned the theatre he performed in as his talent afforded him the right.

If it meant that he had to forego time with his father, Pierre felt it necessary so he would be perfect. As he knew it, his father supported him. He raised him to perform, as he had when he was an able-bodied man, younger, in the prime of his talents; to take great leaps upstage was a most primal desire for Pierre. It was all he'd been told to want. He spun, *en pointe*, long since the silence filled his room, so he heard his papa weeping when he should have been eating his soup. Hunched over his empty bowl, he hid his sorrow behind his hands.

'Papa?' Pierre fell to his knees beside his father, 'Why must you cry? Are you not happy for me?'

He took his father's hands into his own and felt his sadness like it was his own. Some apartment blocks over, there were screams of heavy fighting.

'Please, Pierre, do not go to that theatre anymore.' He said, 'I fear the worst. It is not safe for you to perform anymore. We must leave this place.'

'Papa, please do not ask that of me.' He freed a hand from his father's grip, but his father held tightly onto the other, 'I have to perform. Papa, please do not ask that of me.'

'Why must you perform? Please, Pierre. Please, do not go.'

He started to squeeze his son's hand, so tight that Pierre thought he meant to hurt him. And Pierre needed his hands for his piece, to keep perfect form onstage. He tried to free himself, but his father used all the strength he had to cause his son harm; Pierre had to kick out his father's chair to be free and each fell apart from the other, sprawled out on the patterned carpet.

'Papa!' Pierre pushed off from the carpet, 'Why did you do that, Papa?' On the floor, his father continued to whimper, and because of his immobility it was all he could do but plead.

'I must go. I must finish the piece.'

And so his father would not be left to listen to the artillery as it boomed closer to his apartment, he wound the phonograph so his father could listen through the duration of his accompaniment, and when he left him there he locked the door.

Without his supporting composition, Pierre *pliéd* to the symphony of screaming missiles as they landed nearer the theatre, and threatened his performance. There wasn't an orchestra of strings, yet when he closed his eyes he heard their high rises and flutters to near-silence. And felt his limbs move almost without command. He and the accompaniment became one movement, across-stage and almost into the audience, as they would have soaked up his every move.

Mortar shells rained across the ruins of a city once-thriving. As they totalled the street, Pierre leapt about the stage he commanded in absence of all else. His audience would marvel over all that he could do, as he sissoned upstage, so in tune with his internal rhythm he hadn't noticed the missile as it decimated the theatre front, crumbling into debris. A plume of dust swept upstage and Pierre lost balance, tripped over his other foot. When he landed on his back his arms were spread to *epaulé*.

Again, he heard his accompaniment and leapt up, half-spun upstage, avoided the collapse of what remained of the wings. The grand archway splintered apart and perforated the front row, should they have been seated. Pierre lifted an arm for his audience. There was nothing to sustain but his fouette for the finale. And as the stage separated underfoot, he swirled onstage to what would have been widespread adoration. He heard the orchestral finale in his ears! It was impassioned, fast, and made his heart flutter as he felt it stir him on. Even as heavy weaponry ate stage right, he spiralled through the symphony. And when his foot came down and he raised his arms, straight-backed, there was applause as the theatre came down.

Tal Rejwan

Bad Apples

You think of bad apples,
Rolling from their crates,
Banging on the hard wood floor.

Bang! Bang!

And if you were an apple,
You would be good no more.
But you are not an apple, Snow.
That wasn't just a kiss.

No, no.

You protect your virtue,
You won't be judged by me;
We were all fed bad apples.

And, true, sometimes,
We all feel
The need to hush…
But you're not a bad apple, Snow.

No, no.

You are, in fact,
Not an apple at all.

Tal Rejwan

Circe's Filthy Toys

They felt entitlement,
Over my body,
Over my soul.

With grabby hands
And filthy snots
Touched, marked, hogged.

Who are you,
Little, broken toy?
Not human anymore.

Something to use,
Take apart, toss
No second thought.

Circe was right.
Circe was us,
Filthy little toys.

Tom Robinson

Woden and Odin Take It All In

Seven longships, their bright, painted dragon prows splitting the sea before them. The water parted into waves that rolled and cascaded, only to fall back on themselves and foam and bubble. On the boats their crews, clad in hide and leather and ring mail, heaved on the oars and called out to each other. The sides of the ship were decorated in round shields. Their iron bosses distorting the sea below, and the grey sky overhead.

Land approached.

First a smear of brown and green on the horizon beneath a leaden sky. Then the smear spread. Grew taller. Each detail and each distinction rearing out of the horizon and the ocean itself. A land made anew with their coming, its possibilities endless.

On that new land was a beach. Little more than hardpacked sand and pebbles. The ocean lapped and sucked eagerly at the shore. The wind huffed, scattering salty spray.

And on that beach stood a man.

Tall, broad. A once powerful frame sliding into suet pudding. He wore a grey woollen jumper and a thick duffle coat which he huddled closer into against the cold. The man watched the ships approach through his one, good eye and wished they'd just get on with it so he could find somewhere warm to sit.

Another person strolled down the sands and pebbles towards him. This second figure had watched the first man from the cliffs for a few moments. Looking from him to the ships, to the horizon, and then back again. When he decided it was safe, the second man slid down the cliffside on his heels. His scuffed boots kicking up chalk and pebbles that rattled down onto the beach below.

This second man was leaner, hungrier. His ears pierced from lobe to tip. He wore a creased and faded leather jacket that smelled like a kebab shop in the wee hours of the morning, when all the pubs are closed, and only the sad, befuddled walk home awaits you.

He stopped, a little distance away. Watching. Considering. Then he called out.

'Oi!'

The broad man in his duffle coat twitched but did not turn. His eyes were on the approaching ships, approaching in a loose chevron formation, and on the boat that served as the formation's tip. Its captain now stood on the prow, thumping a meaty fist against his chest while he roared.

'I said oi!'

'What?'

'Don't *what* me. This is my beach. Bugger off.'

'For the moment,' the broad man said with a sigh.

The lean man bore his teeth, marched over, took the broad man by the shoulder and whirled him around. He breathed a miasma of pub carpet and old mustard into the older man's face.

'What you mean "for the moment"?'

'Do I know you?' the broad man said running his one eye over him. The piercings. The sneer. The tattoo of a wide staring eye on the back of his right hand, already turning green around the edges.

'Dunno,' the lean man said, squinting into his face. 'Do I know *you?*'

They studied each other for a moment. The ships crawled closer on the horizon. Up on the cliffs above them, a bell tolled. Someone rang it in a panic while people ran around below, their arms full of precious, glinting things. Hiding them under floor boards. Tossing them into latrine pits. Some prayed. Others watched the horizon in mute horror.

The broad man spoke first, proffering a meaty hand.

'Odin,' he said.

The lean man snorted and shook his head, then shook Odin's hand.

'*Woden,*' he said.

'Oh.'

'Yup.'

'When did you get here?'

'Not that long ago,' Woden said. 'The winters are awful, but the summers aren't too bad. That your lot over there?'

'Afraid so.'

'Got it in their heads to do a bit of plundering?'

Odin nodded his head and turned his eye back to the horizon. Some of the other sailors had abandoned their oars, trusting the current to bring them in, and had joined their captain to shout and cavort and wave their hands about.

'What're they saying?'

Odin closed his one eye and opened the other. When he spoke, it was not in the voice of a man. Imagine the gears of time grinding out each syllable. The bellows of the heavens themselves pushing out the words on the winds of ages.

'*Y! Ylir men. Ae! Aero their. Era mela os. Min warb naseu. Wilr made thaim. I bormotha hauni, I bormotha hauni. Got nafiskr orf. Auim suimade. Foki afa galande, foki afa galande. Hu! War! Hu war Opkam har a hit lot.*'

Odin switched eyes and clucked his tongue. 'A bit on the nose for my taste.'

Woden squinted. 'I feel like I should know that.'

Odin shrugged. 'Something like "old man, cry for the men and women we're going to kill, we've come over the ocean to kill them. Rar rar, aren't we bloody scary."'

'I meant the words. That language,' Woden said, touching a hand to the back of his neck, 'I recognised it even though I didn't know what it meant.'

Odin ran his good eye over him. Behind him, while he looked, the ships grated onto the sands. The sailors took up their shields, donned helmets, drew their weapons, and fell onto the shore in a wave of bellowing, roaring violence. They swept up the incline towards the tolling bell.

'Weird,' Odin said.

'You smoke?' Woden said, offering him a grubby pack that had been sat on more than once. Odin waved him off, so Woden lit one for himself.

'I think they're going to kill your lot,' Odin said.

'Not really my lot. Someone sent them here. For all their preaching and praying and moanin' and whinging, they're better thieves than the both of us. You should see the loot they have up there.'

'I never stole a thing in my life.'

Woden blew a plume of smoke into his face and grinned, his teeth yellow and crooked and cracked.

'Liar.'

Odin smiled, 'You'll never be able to prove it.'

'Yeah, you're probably right.' Woden turned and ran his eye over the cliff and the warriors surging up it, shaking and whirling their weapons overhead whooping and screaming. 'I know I probably shouldn't say this but— you know the ginger one?'

'You're going to have to be more specific.'

'Over there on the right. The one with the finger bones around his neck.'

'Yep, yep, I see him.'

'In about, oh.' Woden jammed the filter between his teeth and see-sawed his head. 'In about four minutes, he's going to go smashing and shrieking into one of the smaller chapels they've got. And there's going to be this guy there. In his forties. Bald like an egg. That guy is going to wet himself as he tries to run, slip in his own puddle, and the ginger guy is going to split his egg with that axe of his.'

'Right?'

'The thing is, baldy is his cousin. I mean, going back a bit now, but ginger's great-uncle got about a bit—'

'Stout feller, looked a bit like a boar having a bad day?'

Woden nodded. 'Beautiful singing voice.'

'I know, right?'

'Well he was gadding about in Francia, right? Whoring, plundering, the usual.'

'What else is there to do down there?'

'I dunno. Buggering horses, but that's not my point. Bloke meets girl. Girl gets pregnant. Gives birth to baldy's dad. Baldy's dad meets girl, cycle repeats, they send baldy off to the mission to get his letters, he ends up being ordained, and here he is.'

'What's your point?'

'My *point*—' Woden stopped. He took the cigarette from his lips. Opened his mouth a few times to speak but ended up closing it when the words failed to appear. 'I dunno what the hell my point was. It's weird, though, right?'

'Maybe to you,' Odin said, 'but some of us have been about a bit—'

'Don't pull that with me old man. Those two up there, they're related. He's going to bash his cousin's brains in and never know the difference. How many more up there are going to do the same?'

'I'd say a good half dozen or so,' Odin said.

Crashes and shouts rolled down the hill towards them. An inky tendril of smoke drifted upward towards the grey sky, thickening as it went. The two of them watched it go.

'That's *weird* though, right?'

Odin shrugged. 'My lot are starving. Winters are harsh. Not enough to go around. Babies freeze to their mothers ti—'

'Don't bring the kids into this, I swear—'

'Who are you going to swear *to*?'

Woden didn't have anything to say to that, so he jammed the cigarette's filter back between his teeth and glowered up towards the smoke. The wind picked up. Whatever fire the warriors had started, it was hungry, and growing fast.

'Fine, fine, no children,' Odin said spreading his hands. 'But the point stands. My lot are hungry. Your lot—'

'They're not *my* lot.'

'It's your beach, isn't it?'

'Well—'

'And they're living right next to it. This is your patch. Your patch, your people. Can I finish?'

Woden shot him a look but said nothing.

'My lot are hungry, your lot aren't. Ipso facto, we're coming to smash your faces in. Cousins or not.'

'Doesn't that bother you a bit, though?' Woden said. 'Like any other time or place, if ginger's uncle had stayed closer to home, ginger and baldy might've been buds.'

'Or they could've killed each other anyway.'

Woden sighed, 'Yeah. But now they'll never know any different.'

'I won't deny that,' Odin said. Then after a few moments, 'Kind of takes all the fun and the romance out of it.'

'There's no dressing it up. Not really. All of this.' Woden waved a hand at the smoke, still coiling ever higher. 'It's a mess. That's what it is. And it'll just get worse.'

'What do you mean?'

'Oh, come off it. As soon as your lot get a look at all the shiny goodies up there, they'll decide to stay. See if anyone's got anything better. Then they'll find out the land here is much gentler and softer than the land back home. They'll bring their families, build houses. Tear down everything that's already here and spread and spread and spread.'

'But isn't that—'

'Yeah I know. I'm aware of the sodding hypocrisy of it. But still. Then in about eighty or ninety years' time, some king will pop his clogs, one of my lot will decide he's king, at exactly the same point someone in Francia decides the exact same thing.'

'So they'll fight it out. So what?'

'Except that Francian bloke is related to my bloke. The Francian bloke's soldiers are all related to my soldiers, and then when they're done with my lot they'll go North and kill your lot.'

Odin scowled for a moment, 'But my lot settled there first. They're only there because—'

'They don't care. Pop up a few walls. Build a house. Say this is mine, that's yours, and voila—you've got the makings of a war. As soon as you pop that wall up, your neighbour—hell they could be your brother—once the walls gone up, you get to thinking they could be doing *anything* over there.'

'Right.'

'And so you says to yourself, "I bet that bastard is plotting something. He wants what I've got. Well I'll sort him. I'll sort him good." Then you pop over the wall, smash his face in, and sleep soundly that night. Because the moment you built that wall, he's not your brother anymore.'

Odin sighed through his nose and shoved his hands in his pockets.

A monk, no more than a boy really, tumbled down the cliffside towards them. A jagged red line down the front of his habit. The black wool turning ochre. He'd been running, and tripped, and now he was going to fall to the beach and die.

Woden stepped aside, to make way for him.

When the boy landed in a cloud of sand and scattered pebbles, spreading a crimson stain on the ground below, Odin sighed again.

'It doesn't seem anywhere near as fun anymore,' he said.

Woden nodded, and the two of them looked down at the fallen youth. The sea breeze ruffled his hair. Tousling it, by way of farewell. Above them a ginger beard jutting beneath an iron helmet peered over the cliffs edge. Saw the fallen boy, saw the beach, and nothing else. The beard and the helmet withdrew.

'Wish I hadn't come,' Woden said at last.

'Why did you?'

'This is going to sound really stupid.'

'Go on.'

'Thought you might've been my dad.'

Odin laughed, 'Don't be daft. Not unless you—'

He opened both his eyes and stared into the younger man's face.

'Oh, balls,' Odin breathed.

Kübra Sevim

Devil's Night

I fell at her feet as though dead,
She had denied us Heaven and Earth
Free reign and left us without form.
Darkness was upon the face of the beasts.
We called her Malum,
And Malum said, 'Let there be evil: and there was evil.'
Evil had overtaken light and left no day,
And this was the first day.

She said, 'Let death live and reside in the midst of man and let it divide the good from the bad
Leaving only the bad.'
She said, 'Let the sins be gathered together unto one place, and let the bloody party commence' And it was so.

'Let the beasts and creatures bring forth mischievous fun.
Let the dead walk and the darkness rule, lets show them thrill'
And this was only the beginning of the second day.

And Malum said, 'Let the creatures bring forth torture upon the newcomers, the evil yielding seed.
Seed their food, make them evil, make them cackle.' And on the third day,
Malum saw that they were made deadly.

And Malum said, 'Let there be darkness in the perdition of Hell,
Let blood flood the boring good of Earth, and drown man's skin
Scorch their flesh and make them Hell's Earthlings.
Bring them to the party.' And it was so,
And the evening of the party was the fourth day.

Malum created soulless beasts and avenged the greatest of sinners
They devoured a feast of human flesh and got drunk from fermented human blood.
And so it was called 'The Night of the Living Dead', the great party of Devils.
And so Malum welcomed us to the fun house, and this was the fifth day.

Malum saw that there were no rules.
She said, 'Let Hell bring forth our most evil creature
Let us recreate in its image.
Let us all give into our dark temptations: let sin ravage us, let us be free.'
And so Malum had blessed us with some real fun: I have now come to know,

Lo and behold, she was the creator of the most evil fun, a creator of an Earthless life, the walking dead.
And on the sixth day we were officially at the beginning of the end.

Michelle Stoddart

The Earth is a Harlot

Scene 1:

Int. Bedroom.
(*Speaker stands far centre stage. in front of them, a Man and a Woman. they dance, almost ethereally, like the memory of home. Man and Woman can interact with Speaker, if so — Speaker is sarcastically inclined towards Man and gently kind to Woman. Speaker holds a clear fear of the bed that sits at centre stage, covered in soot.*)

Speaker:
extinction, noun.
meaning, the state or process of being or becoming extinct.
oh, how familiar she is with this client who wears his liar's crown.
succinctly loving, wholly unbound.

he finds her in the cornerstone of everything,
her god of liars, pathetically marked with the last sting
of bountiful pollination.
a ghostly reminder of her lovely dead friend,
unfortunate spring.

he is dressed in a boilersuit,
stained in blackberry smog and cherry wine flames
a generously paying brute, seeking to tame,
the forged harlot.

she takes the wolfish form of a creature that will never reach the next century,
once wildly complimentary,
now a bureaucratic accessory.
the irony is sadly exemplary.

and she is choking!
choking, on lipstick dyed with pollution.
croaking out a wait, wait!
seeking naive absolution.
yet it is too late, far far too late.

they collide,
a familiar waltz.
her ribbon-cut morsels of salvation,
swallowed by his maw of dismayed attribution.

he never wanted;
to taste,
to hold,
to suffocate,
to drag her into a deathly threshold.
she was a summertime companion,
not an empty canyon,
for his indulgent pleasure.

yet they collide still,
fusing—
melting—
becoming—
a monstrous folklore.

and she is losing!
losing, to a man who never wanted to win.
wheezing out I know, I know.
tasting his smoky tears,
feeling the virus in her begin to sow, sow.

he braces against her, sobbingly begging why.
why these mortals,
sadistically inclined.
bruise your delicate landscape,
and blacken your fragile blue sky.

but he is man-made,
machine-raised.
he does not remember he sits on the throne,
where these mortals wantonly pray.

yet how could she have known?
the inventors of her own gallows,
artists of her ballad of woe.

were the same friends
who were once her gentle Juliets
and brave Romeos.

and she is crying!
wailing,
she is dying!

but her calls are ignored,
her children are long buried.
by the ones who now carry,
the names more foul,
than the hope for another tomorrow.

she is a harlot,
a whore.
who sold herself for a chance for another summer.
haunted,
by amputees
who used to hold the sky with and call themselves a forest.
plagued,
by oceans that have become bottled wine.
cursed,
by the sight of gulls fleeing into the earth to become feathered worms.

these regrets strike her, tearing at her gown
demanding.
help, help, help.

yet she still lies underneath a man,
who is strung by puppeteers,
of men and women,
who deny
that they are killing themselves.

(*exit MAN. SPEAKER hesitantly walks to WOMAN, who shakes her head and smiles comfortingly. SPEAKER clearly does not want to leave WOMAN. SPEAKER slowly approaches WOMAN, as if their presence would make her shatter. they kneel beside the bed, as if worshipping WOMAN.*)

WOMAN:

i never expected that my body would be such a travesty.

(*SPEAKER bows their head, sullen. WOMAN stares upwards, beautifully basking in her own tears.*)

SPEAKER:

we never meant to hurt you like this.

WOMAN:

you always are. sorry today, glad tomorrow. i have heard a thousand excuses and seen a million denials. tell me, little bard. do they pity me?

(*SPEAKER clearly is uncomfortable from the question. there is a long indeterminate pause. WOMAN eventually laughs, brokenly lovely.*)

WOMAN:

no. i did not think they were.

SPEAKER:

some do! i — i do!

WOMAN:

yet you are all swallowed in the maw of wolfish men and vulturous women. i see it so, a prophecy of futility where I'll be crowned with tragedy.

SPEAKER:

we'll climb out of their teeth—

WOMAN:

and leave me behind.

SPEAKER:

stop this pessimistic nonsense! we'll get you out of there, i promise—

WOMAN:

promises, they are the colour of forget-me-nots. you truly think i have not heard this before, valiant poet? the sands of time always offers me a new mortal who makes me dream of another century, but now the sandstorm has found me and i am tired of running.

SPEAKER:

then i'll find a cave for you to hide and rest. to recover your strength! and
when you trick the reaper of oblivion i'll find you, i'll hold your hand, and
we will walk into another century. together.

(*WOMAN smiles.*)

WOMAN:

witty writer, i am long gone. at this very moment my last century has
approached me with a heavy heart, and the song of your people.

(*enter ENSEMBLE. each member is dressed differently to mimic positions of power.
they each hold an air of arrogance and smarmy nature.*)

SPEAKER:
my people?

WOMAN:

yes, my soft-hearted artist. your people, they sing a song of my death. and
they sing it very well.

(*SPEAKER tries to drag WOMAN away as ENSEMBLE crowd around them.*)

SPEAKER:

no. no. no, come with me!

WOMAN:

no. i can't, bold actor. this is the grave i shall be buried in.

SPEAKER:

th- this bed? you call this a grave? no, this is a shrine of abuse! and these
people, they are more monster than man! they are violating your chance of
hope, singing tunes that drown you in despair. they would rather unearth
your soul and use your vacant body to offer to the gods of technology
and fumes. no, no. you do *not* deserve this. you deserve *more* than we *ever*
gave you.

(*ENSEMBLE crawls onto the bed, SPEAKER rushes to them. they collide, fighting
savagely. SPEAKER struggles against them, yelling with fury as ENSEMBLE throws
them off the bed and begin embracing WOMAN hungrily. SPEAKER tries to fight*

through the mutated form, but the efforts are futile. WOMAN'S *face is all that is left of her.*)

WOMAN:

kind architect stop fighting. leave it for another day. go, while the air is still clean here. find another part of me, untouched. give that place a sense of strength.

SPEAKER:

i won't leave you!

WOMAN:

you must. the air is dry and i will not see your lovely bones grow with black flowers.

SPEAKER:

there must be another way!

WOMAN:

those ran out eons ago when coal was married to flame.

(SPEAKER *is dismayed, on the edge of crying with abandon.*)

SPEAKER:

please.

WOMAN:

go.

(ENSEMBLE *begins to grin in sync, disturbingly robotic as they offer* SPEAKER *to join with clawed hands.*)

ENSEMBLE:

stay. stay, where the grass is obsidian and the sky is plastic. pristinely ordinate, perfectly balanced. join us, won't you? little one?

WOMAN:

go!

(SPEAKER *cries openly, wailing like a child who has lost their mother. they stagger towards* ENSEMBLE, *but* WOMAN *pushes him away with the last fragments of strength she had.*)

WOMAN:

make this world kinder, brighter. make me dance with the breeze once more and sing with the mountains. make the rivers paint again and my old friends leave their status as mythology. make me live to see another summertime. leave. *leave!*

(SPEAKER *falls to the floor, reaching as* WOMAN *disappears completely.* ENSEMBLE *laughs wildly, insanely. it clearly scares* SPEAKER, *who stands in fright.* ENSEMBLE *mockingly sings as they move, the sick amalgamation makes* SPEAKER *shriek in fright as it prowls closer to them.*)

ENSEMBLE:

little child
of sweet summertime
missing the earthly mother
embrace us
join us
we will love you still
despite you being
a silver tongue
that promises better lives
for the next century
of childish will.

SPEAKER:

no. no i will not join—

ENSEMBLE:

then perish
poet of earth.
in our black flames
and white plagues.
you think the powerful will listen?
no they kneel.
to forces like us,
who dictate their will.

SPEAKER:
they will listen to me.

ENSEMBLE:
noose. noose
it will always be a noose.
whether be by society or mental,
your naive mouth,
will choke on your naive truth.

SPEAKER:
then i'll choke. we all will, until the rich suffocate no longer and help the
poor.

ENSEMBLE:
and if they don't little fool?

SPEAKER:
…then at least we are all buried in the same ground.

(*exit SPEAKER*).

Simon Everett, Melissa Shales
Acknowledgements

An anthology is only as successful as the sum of its parts and so it is only right that thanks must first be paid to the authors who kindly submitted their work to be published here — each submission bold, carefully wrought, and with something important to say. Thank you, each of you, for your wonderful contributions.

This edition of *Creel* is the first to have been selected, edited and typeset by University of Essex students from across the Department of Literature, Film and Theatre Studies. The amount of commitment, dedication, and ingenuity that the editorial team has displayed throughout the production of *Creel 5* has been outstanding. Many thanks must go to each of them for their efforts; this has been an intense but rewarding learning experience for them over the course of many months.

Special thanks should be given to Ezgi Gürhan, the Editor-in-Chief of this anthology, for taking such a strong lead, coordinating the editorial process with determination and skill. Our cover artist, Tal Rejwan, should also be thanked for her fantastic artwork that enfolds the cover of this publication. Further acknowledgements must go to Dr Simon Everett of Muscaliet Press, who guided the students, aided in part by Melissa Shales, offering them the opportunity to hone their abilities as both writers and publishers.

Thanks must also be given to the Department of Literature, Film and Theatre Studies for allowing students to undertake this opportunity, one which will serve both the authors and editors well in their future endeavours. The Head of Department, Professor Elizabeth Kuti, must be thanked both for her illuminating and passionate foreword to the anthology; and for being such a supportive figure throughout the publication's twists and turns.

****

It has been a real pleasure for Muscaliet Press to be involved in the publication of *Creel 5*: from the germination of the theme of the anthology, to the call for submissions and selection stage, right through to the copyedit, and finally layout phase.

Producing a publication is not an easy task, and working with so many writers and editors can present complex hurdles to overcome. However, it is a feat of strength that this anthology has come together against a backdrop of external disruption and adversity; for that, I want to emphasise that everyone who has been involved with *Creel 5* should be extremely proud of what has been accomplished in the little time that we have had available to us.

In better times, I hope you can all look fondly back on this anthology as an example of what is possible even when the world outside is bleak, and that in such bleakness holding onto your passion for writing should be privileged, and cherished.

Dr Simon Everett
Editor-in-Chief, Muscaliet Press
Colchester; April 2020

About the Authors

Tom Allpress studies BA Literature and Creative Writing at the University of Essex. His writing interests are in free-form poetry, formally experimental writing, such as Oulipo and haiku, and screenwriting. This will be the first time he has been published.

Nathan Ashby is studying BA Creative Writing at the University of Essex. He often writes poetry and occasionally short descriptive prose. His two favourite genres are horror and comedy.

Ann Berry is a second year undergraduate in Creative Writing at the University of Essex. After a career overseas that involved much travelling, she is interested in Ancient Greece, travel writing and psychogeography.

Karenza Bolton is currently studying MA Literature at the University of Essex after completing a BA in English Literature at Oxford Brookes University in 2019. She lives in Chelmsford with her family.

Roseanne Ganley is currently studying for a PhD at the University of Essex. She is interested in posthuman thought, speculative fiction and nature writing and has published an essay on '*The Cyberflaneur in the Age of Digital Technology*' in the *Essex Student Research Online* (ESTRO) journal.

Harry Hughes is a MA Creative Writing student, who was previously published in two anthologies during his time at the University of Essex. He has an interest in poetry, abstract and surrealist theory and is the current president of the University's Writing Society, who is currently editing their own anthology.

Daniel Jeffrey's stories have appeared in *AMBIT, The London Magazine, LITRO, The Lampeter Review* and *Esquire*. He is currently studying for a PhD in vampire literature where the life is no longer in the blood.

Petra McQueen is a writer and teacher. Her writing has appeared in *The Saturday Evening Post, The Guardian* and *You Magazine*, among many other publications. She has won several prizes for her prose, including first prize in the National Association of Writers' Groups' Short Story Competition. She lives close to the mud-flats of North East Essex, UK with her large, lively family. She runs her own writing workshops (www.thewriterscompany. co.uk), and is currently working on her PhD at the University of Essex.

Adam Neikirk is a PhD student in Creative Writing at the University of Essex. He is interested in the intersection of contemporary culture with historical poetic forms and Romantic sensibility of the 18th and 19th centuries. His dissertation comprises a long poem about the Romantic poet Samuel Taylor Coleridge.

Robert Newman is in his second year of studying BA Creative Writing and English Literature at the University of Essex. He is interested in exploring human psychology and the underbelly of society through creative prose.

Jordan Reddington is currently studying BA Creative Writing at the University of Essex. He is interested in the use of literature to explore societal norms and forces of oppression.

Tom Robinson is a first year Creative Writing research student at the University of Essex. He has one short story published by the British Fantasy Society, *On Well-Wishers* (Vol. 8, 2019). Currently resides in Colchester with his wife, Hollie, and son Hunter. Writes Fantasy stories and other nonsense.

Kübra Sevim is currently studying English Literature and Creative Writing at the University of Essex. She is interested in a variety of writing styles and hopes to write a novel.

Michelle Lèon Stoddart is a BA Literature and Creative Writing student at the University of Essex, working towards an MA. Her current interests are postmodern literature and psychoanalytic theory. Her favourite work is *The Strange Case of Dr. Jekyll and Mr. Hyde* by Robert Louis Stevenson.

About the Editors

Hannah Bransom is a first year student working towards her bachelor's degree in Literature and Creative Writing. She is passionate about all forms of writing and is particularly interested in shorter forms, such as poems and novellas.

Loren Ennis is a fourth year English Literature student at the University of Essex. She specialises in Children's Literature and Shakespeare and is interested in literature about mythology and fantasy.

Simon Everett is Editor-in-Chief of Muscaliet Press; he is also a poet and poet-translator. His latest poetry collection, *Tamám* (Litmus Publishing, forthcoming), is an experimental reinterpretation of *The Rubáiyát of Omar Khayyám*; and his translations of Chinese T'ang dynasty poetry have been published in *STAND* magazine and *Chinese Arts and Letters journal*. He holds a PhD in Creative Writing from the University of Essex, funded by the Consortium for the Humanities and the Arts South-East England (CHASE). Simon also held the position of Layout Editor for the *Brief Encounters* CHASE journal from 2017-2019.

Saffron Forde is a determined Literature and Creative Writing student at the University of Essex, in the early stages of becoming a successful editor.

Sam 'Jesta' Geden is a film-maker, writer and performer studying MA Film at the University of Essex. He is also a passionate academic and practitioner of stereoscopy, having given lectures on the topic to the Stereoscopic Society and in several university modules. His work has previously been published by the University of Essex Writing Society, the London Stereoscopic Company and *QueenOnline*, and was shortlisted for the Screen South 2020 New Creatives audio drama development scheme.

Ezgi Gürhan is a BA Literature and Creative Writing student at the University of Essex. She is interested in philosophy, history and mythology. She likes to rewrite myths and fairy tales. Her favourite genre is fantasy.

Fanny Haushalter is currently a first year at the University of Essex and she is studying BA Literature and Creative Writing. It is her first published work.

Sophie Jeans is a second year creative writing student at the University of Essex. Her work is mostly in poetry and microfiction and hopes to work further in publishing.

Jennifer Li is studying BA Film and Creative Writing at (you guessed it) the University of Essex. As a first-year, she is interested in writing comedy and drama. She would like to thank her mother and brother for their never-ending support.

Cristina del Pozo Huertas is currently studying first year of BA English Language and Literature at the University of Essex. She is interested in fantasy and magical realism and draws inspiration from her mother country, Spain. She has previously published short stories in two anthologies called *Punto y seguido* (2016) and *VTT* (Vicios de Transmisión Textual) (2017).

Tal Rejwan is a BA Creative Writing student at the University of Essex. She previously worked in Graff Publishing House as a social media manager, and illustrated book covers for Adel Publishing in Israel. She was a panellist and a lecturer in ICon and Olamot festivals in Israel. Her artwork has been featured at the 2019 International Erotic Art Exhibition in London.

Melissa Shales BA Hons WC FRGS AFHEA is a writer, editor and publisher, author of around thirty books and many hundreds of articles. She is currently completing a PhD in Creative Writing in the LiFTS Dept at the University of Essex.

Minn Yap is in her second year at the University of Essex studying Literature and Creative Writing. She is aiming to become an editor at a publishing house after graduation, and hopes her literary skills and experience in The Publishing Project: *Creel 5* will help her progress in her goals.